FLASHCARDS
AND
THE CURSE OF AMBROSIA

FLASHCARDS
AND
THE CURSE OF AMBROSIA

NOVELLAS

BY TRACY ROBERT

MANY VOICES PROJECT
AWARD WINNER #131

Cover design by Rolf Busch
Interior design by Daniel Arthur Shudlick
Author photo by Kerry Krenzin

The publication of *Flashcards and The Curse of Ambrosia* is made possible by
the generous support of Minnesota State University Moorhead,
The McKnight Foundation, the Dawson Family Endowment, Northern
Lights Library Network, and other contributors to New Rivers Press.

For copyright permission, please contact Frederick T. Courtright
at 570-839-7477 or permdude@eclipse.net.

New Rivers Press is a nonprofit literary press associated with
Minnesota State University Moorhead.

Alan Davis, Co-Director and Senior Editor
Suzzanne Kelley, Co-Director and Managing Editor
Kevin Carollo, MVP Poetry Coordinator
Vincent Reusch, MVP Prose Coordinator
Thom Tammaro, Poetry Editor
Nayt Rundquist, Assistant Production Editor
Wayne Gudmundson, Consultant

Publishing Interns:
Kjersti Maday, Kelly Mead, Mikaila Norman

Flashcards and The Curse of Ambrosia Book Team:
Adam Barone, Marcus Bjornson, Bryce Erdmann, Elizabeth Wester

∞   Printed in the USA using acid-free, archival-grade paper.
Flachcards & The Curse of Ambrosia is distributed nationally by
Small Press Distribution.

New Rivers Press
c/o MSUM
1104 7th Avenue South
Moorhead, MN 56563
www.newriverspress.com

For my brother Matt

Contents

Flashcards

Prologue: Braceros	1
Flashcards	7
An Inspired Break	17
Queen of the Tree of the Dead	27
Badness Is a Calling	31
The Great Void	45
Deviled Eggs	57
The Imperviousness of Elbow Skin	63
The Core	67

The Curse of Ambrosia

Prologue: The Curse	89
Eggs in Viable Shells	93
Live Ones	103
Who Knew	111
Final Level of Protection	125
Hearts, Crazy Eights, and Old Maid	133
Questions and Answers	145
The Few Worldly Blessings	155
Tie Breaker	161

Acknowledgments
About the Author
About New Rivers Press

FLASHCARDS

The blood is checkered by
so many stains and wishes . . .
—Delmore Schwartz

PROLOGUE: *BRACEROS*

BEFORE LIQUOR, MY MOTHER INDULGED in her hi-fi. She had a record collection of which she kept scrupulous care with rubbing alcohol and a velvet cloth.

Between our kitchen and living room was a six-by-three window without glass, a hand-through for food and drink. We seldom used the passageway for that purpose, but my mother's hi-fi faced the kitchen, and the hand-through formed a conduit of sound for the records stacked on the turntable. As she cooked and cleaned, she listened to Broadway musicals, folk songs, popular recording artists: Nat King Cole, Frank Sinatra, Perry Como, Ella Fitzgerald. My mother didn't sing or hum along; the music set her chores to a bearable rhythm. Three decades later, I can't hear Rex Harrison or Richard Burton's voice without conjuring Henry Higgins and King Arthur—those men prettified by musical theatre and undone by glorious plans.

Some musical selections, I noticed, urged my mother to tears. A Kingston Trio record, eventually unplayable from overuse, included a Woody Guthrie song that always made her weep: "Deportee." When I had the vocabulary, I asked why she would choose to listen to a song that saddened her.

She looked at my face from eye to eye. On her hip, she bounced my brother, Pierce, a toddler then with an oblong and virtually bald head. This was the first time my mother stalled over a question of mine.

"I'm not sure, honey. It's about hard-working people sent back to Mexico. They die in a plane crash on their way home and aren't even buried with their names. Maybe I cry for them because that's as much as I can do."

Pierce batted at her long pageboy. "Hair, hair, hair," he announced. I doubted if he'd ever have hair of his own, or make any kind of sense, and I couldn't imagine why my mother pledged so many tears to people whose identities were unknown.

❀ ❀ ❀ ❀

Late spring of the year I started kindergarten, a listing flatbed truck stacked with wooden crates appeared on our manicured street. Amid crates in the back of a separate pickup were dozens of men, most of them shorter than my father. Their skin, though, was the same brown he turned in the summer when he spent time at the beach, the color of the wheat bread toast I insisted on having for breakfast because I could prepare it myself.

"Mom," I said. "Who are those men? Why do they have aprons on sideways?"

She laughed. "They only look like aprons because they're not full of fruit yet. The men are *braceros*, Phoebe, here to pick grapefruit and oranges."

"Own-jeth, own-jeth." Pierce's word celebrations made my ears itch. I left the kitchen to get ready for school.

That afternoon, I slouched against the beige stucco outside my bedroom and watched. Braceros swarmed over trees as bees had earlier in the year when the leaves were dotted with white blossoms, sweetening the air of the neighborhood. Workers scurried up and down ladders, filling their shoulder sacks, emptying them into crates. A special squadron of men hauled the heavy crates out to the truck and alternated turns resting after trips. One bracero chose the shade of the tree nearest my room as his break site. He sat on a prickly cushion of leaves and took a penknife from his dungaree pocket, then peeled the top half of a grapefruit and ate it as if it were a snow cone. I'd never seen a person consume a grapefruit in this way, my stare rude with curiosity.

The man peeled another grapefruit in the same fashion and held it out to me. Gold shone around his front teeth, and I thought his smile was beautiful.

"Thank you, bracero," I said, accepting the fruit.

He glowered at me slightly, then his face softened. "*Ernesto*," he said. "*Mi llamo es Ernesto*." He punched at his chest with his index finger. "Me," he said. "Ernesto."

"Oh," I said, pointing to myself. "Me, Phoebe."

He extended a sticky, calloused hand that I shook, and I sat in the leaves next to him, munching the tangy confection.

Ernesto produced a silver coin of a design I did not recognize, and made it disappear. He displayed his hands, palm and back, pulled behind his ear, and retrieved the coin, scratching his head as if baffled by the discovery. I giggled at his showmanship, while Ernesto continued to lose the coin and find it in alarming places: his mouth, beneath the leaves, in midair, and finally, in my nose. I began a staccato laugh of delight and surprise, choking on a piece of grapefruit.

My breath didn't immediately come to me, so Ernesto put me on my feet, and rubbed and slapped at my back to jar the pulp loose. In Spanish, he murmured words whose comforting intent I fully understood. At this moment, my mother, reacting to my gagging laughter, peered out the bedroom window. Soon the scuff of her pink and yellow terrycloth slippers summoned me.

Ernesto rose and inclined his head in her direction. "*Buenos tardes, Señora*," he said, the playfulness gone from his eyes, no trace of the showman in his posture. He reminded me of the sparkling life in tide pools—maroon hermit crabs, silvery-green sea anemones, violet limpets— that shrank into itself for protection.

"*Buenos tardes*," my mother said, and she made the warm language seem cold. She gripped my shoulder—by then, entirely absorbed by my mother's effect on Ernesto, I'd stopped choking—and steered me toward the door. I swerved to wave at him, but he was shaking his head at the ground, returning the coin to his pocket.

Pierce, awake in his crib, belted out a nonsense tune as if to add to my confusion. "Go-kee, go-bee, go-ree, PAAAH."

My mother yelled down the hallway, "Night-night, Pierce. Sleep."

She grabbed my grapefruit cone and threw it in the garbage pail under the sink, wet a dishtowel, and scoured my face and hands. She spoke in the rapid, breathy voice that meant she was upset and trying to conceal it.

"Phoebe, you must not accept food from people you don't know. Ever."

"The fruit was from our own tree," I sputtered through the cloth. "In our yard."

Her voice grew breathier. "You mustn't talk to a bracero when he's supposed to be working. They move too quickly. You have to stay out of the way, or you could trip and send braceros and fruit and bags flying . . ."

"Mother, he had a magic coin. And he isn't called bracero. His name is Ernesto."

The dishcloth dropped to the imitation brick linoleum. "Oh my God," she said, the calm of her face breaking like a delicate shell. "My dear, interfering God."

She opened a cupboard and poured into a glass the liquid that smelled like cologne mixed with something rotten. She put ice and soda in the glass too, and sat at the kitchen table.

The house went still, as though it listened to her thoughts; Pierce at least contemplated a nap. I waited for what I considered a wise duration, then asked my mother for a sip.

"No," she said.

I asked why not.

"Because children can't drink what I'm drinking." She took the glass to the master bedroom and closed the door.

My father's briefcase swung onto the table, where I waited for and worried about my mother.

"Sandra?" he called, winking cheerily at me. "Sandra, sweetheart, I'm home. Back from the Crusades." I directed him down the hall.

My mother wept at the sight of him, and I crept close to listen. "I'd rather not be a mother," she said.

"You're drinking, Sandra." There was hesitant relief in how he exhaled the words. "When you drink you're overly sensitive."

"I'm always overly sensitive," she brusquely replied. "I just don't let you see it."

❀ ❀ ❀ ❀

Our dinner rang with civility: "Please pass . . ." and "Would you like more . . ." and "Yes, please," and "No, thank you." Pierce shoved a hand, all but the thumb, in his mouth, his dollops of eyes following the spectacle of plates and arms and cautious voices. I felt a twinge of belief that he was my brother. Maybe he couldn't talk, but he could see.

After dinner, my mother played the "Deportee" side of the Kingston Trio album over and over. Wary of her need for privacy, I kept distant in the hallway. She knelt between the couch and the coffee table, the glow of her cigarette answering the hi-fi light across the darkened room.

Flashcards

This is Woodland Hills: ground floor castles in basin fog, the grainy light of television in their windows. A yacht built in a tight backyard will eventually be lifted out by crane. Peacocks and a monkey shriek and yowl. I once saw a patio set drift down a poorly planned avenue when the rains came, always a surprise in Southern California, as well as drought. On king-size beds, parents sleep the proud, dazed slumber of success while teenagers discover sex on the carpet of their fathers' studies. I don't know this yet, though. I'm nine.

These are my parents, children of the Depression. My father is a fifth-grade teacher, about-to-be principal. He has a head of wavy dark hair, is tall and muscular, a summer lifeguard. He tells his students and my brother and me that grades don't matter, so long as you do your best. On the rare occasions we bring home Bs, his philosophy stays at the workplace, and there are flashcards. My mother is blonde, long-waisted, swan-necked, gorgeous. She tap danced into designer modeling, modeled my father's way through college. She had an agent and was about to audition for her first speaking role when my father asked her to choose between motherhood and stardom. Homemaking, she says, is the hardest job she's ever landed, and she approaches it like science. Lemon oil for cedar paneling, cabinets, hardwood furniture. No waxy scum. Chlorine cleanser for tile and porcelain because the pine-scented products remind her of truck stops. She's a connoisseur of casseroles.

"What do you think, too runny? Should've taken the lid off sooner? Here, let me drain some of the soup."

"For crying out loud, Sandra," my father says. "Will you quit your fussing and sit down at this dinner table?"

Where we gather for food is *this* dinner table, not *our* table, not *the.* My father refers to the table emphatically, as if it were a shrine and could magically unite us. It's covered with a floor-length skirt of muslin and a square calico bib, both my mother's handiwork. My brother, who's six, pinches my ankle with his prehensile toes.

"Ow. Cut it out, you creature."

"Phoebe," my father says. "There'll be no name calling at this table."

"What a chop, what a burn," my brother says.

"Enough, all of you." My mother, maintaining the gloss of her home. "Straighten up and eat your succotash."

"Thuffering thoccotath." This is Pierce. He has a butch haircut, enormous red ears, and a lisp he exaggerates for attention. He visits the school speech therapist once a week and is supposed to practice enunciating *steam shovel* at night in front of the mirror. He has a white rat named Babushka. She wraps around his neck and gnaws his T-shirt collars ragged. He, in turn, annihilates her name. Pierce often sings "Waltzing Matilda" to the rat, and replaces the song's given name with hers. He hopes someday to work for the United Nations.

This is my father's study, which he calls a den because it's sunken, our house split-level. My father plans lessons here, grades papers, writes the dissertation for his doctorate in education. He has a built-in bookcase, swivel chair, huge oak desk with a compartment that pulls out and up like a tiny trundle bed on which he keeps the Smith Corona we're forbidden to touch. Above the desk is an etching of JFK, with his "Ask not..." quote taped to the glass. My mother bought it as a victory token in honor of the campaign they worked passionately for. My father added the words. He makes sure what goes into the den bears his name, his mark, even the gift from his wife.

At the side of the house, between the kitchen and the garage, is my mother's laundry room, but for some reason she calls it the back porch. In here, she's a true chemist. Liquid and powdered bleaches and detergents, starch, soda, softener, and stain remover. Piles for lights and darks and brights. Separate receptacles for each of our finished clothes, names painted in nail polish on the tubs. She spends as much time in this room as my father does his den, which could be why she calls her place the back porch. It sounds welcoming and homey. In a few years, she'll stash a gin bottle amid her numerous laundry aids.

This is the door of my parents' bedroom, a heavy door, solid. They've attached a full-length mirror to the other side of it to make it heavier. When the door is closed, it means stay out, except on Sundays, when we're allowed to loll on their giant bed and read the funnies. Pierce and I don't fight, these mornings in their room; we sense the privilege might easily be revoked.

Finally, this is Monday, the day I almost died. It approximates legend in my old neighborhood because I sprawled unconscious in the street for nearly an hour in broad daylight, bleeding from my elbows, knees, and nose until a stranger found me.

❀ ❀ ❀ ❀

I came home from school. I ate a carton of peach yogurt. My father deemed it good for me, a health food, but I didn't care for the sour taste. I liked the color, fleshy and bland as a pinup girl from a movie poster. I changed into my turquoise pedal pushers and crop top. In the backyard, the late October heat and grinding noise were oppressive. Dirty, shirtless, sunburned men gunited the trough at the edge of our lot. The word *gunite* spoke to me of combat; the trunk of the orange tree I leaned on vibrated from the roar. The pool wouldn't be lagoon-shaped or graceful as my mother desired, but my father's no-nonsense rectangle for swimming laps.

Behind me on the lawn, Pierce was in costume despite the heat wave: Davy Crockett hat, buckskin jacket that framed his concave chest and distended navel, Tahitian print swim shorts, cowboy boots with tin spurs. He marched in circles, hollered the lyrics of Babushka's song, straining for the high notes, pumping her up and down in the seat of his hand. His rat the grand marshal, he celebrated the pool with a parade.

Someone slugged me on the shoulder: Webb Harttrick, a boy in my class, lured by the din of machinery, Pierce flanking him in defense of our turf. Webb was the first boy to pay me a home call, and a new instinct told me not to slug him back. A head taller than he was, I might've flattened him.

"Loud," he said, inspecting his black sneakers.

"Who are you?" Pierce said, ears aflame, holding Babushka in front of him like a talisman.

"Weird brother." With a sideways thumb, he indicated Pierce.

"Demented," I said, thinking better of it. Webb wasn't in my reading group.

"Minted?" In a deft and vaguely hostile motion, he dipped his head and flipped his hair back, smoothing it with his hand.

I poked at my temple. "Psycho. Loony."

Pierce got his wounded look, eyes wet and empty brown marbles. "Shoot, Phoebe, who yorked in your eggplant?" The joke had its origins in one of my mother's casseroles. He played for family loyalty.

"None of your business, tongue thrust," I said. He draped the rat over his shoulder, caressed her, resumed a halfhearted march.

"Ha," Webb said. "Big hairy mouse." Stupid. I knew he was stupid, but explained to him the branches of the rodent family. Rats, mice, squirrels, even beavers. Big teeth, as in ro-*dent*, as in *dent*ist, different bodies.

"Can we do something?" Webb was bored, so I gave him the tour I'd taken, usually alone, our modest house in the midst of scandal and splendor. The neighbors on our right sent their children to private school. They also kept peacocks, which warned the owner, a shady entrepreneur, when intruders rattled his gate. I described the birds' cries as the sound of a dozen babies being strangled. I recounted the evening a police car whisked the man away, accused of hiring gunmen to pepper office buildings. He owned a plate glass company and would dispatch a truck to the scene the next day.

"Would not," Webb said. "No family man would do that."

I fought my reputation as teacher's pet, eloquent outcast, person not to be trusted, my one friend a neighbor girl in another class at school. I knew myself as someone who understood what many of her classmates failed to, wronged and smug in her detachment. "He did, I swear."

"Swear on your mother's honor."

I did, then I showed him our neighbors on the left who had a Mexican spider monkey named Tokyo Rose. Our chain-link fence formed part of her cage. I gave her my index finger, which she took in a death grip, fixing me with sympathetic eyes. I didn't tell him the hours I spent just so, talking to her because she appeared to listen. I pointed out the imposing carcass of a yacht beyond her cage. The neighbor, a chiropractor who hung garlic necklaces around his sons when they were crusty-nosed with colds, planned to sail around the world. "Noah's ark," I said.

"Dumb boat." Webb bombed it with a dirt clod. "It'll sink in the harbor." He watched me stroke the monkey's chin. "She looks kind of like your relative. Let's ride bikes."

I was tempted to instruct him on the theory of evolution—she was our relative, she was mankind's relative, and so on. Instead, I ran to tell my mother I was leaving.

In the kitchen, she contemplated a can of hollandaise. Her fragile neck tilted and straightened. "Does this can look dented to you, or swollen?"

"Dented, kind of like it got dropped." At such times, I was short with her, as though I were a mother answering her infantile questions. Who cared about a can of white sauce?

"I certainly didn't drop it. You didn't drop it. I can't recall it ever being dropped. Of course, it might've been dropped at the store, or en route to the store." She pondered the possibilities, and I sighed at the mental energy she exerted, as if the can had descended from outer space into our pantry. "Oh well," she said, cranking the opener. "So I contaminate my family."

"I'm going on a ride with a boy, Webb, from school."

She stopped mid-crank. A strange, emboldened glaze crossed her fine features. Her voice lost its quizzical lilt. She said, very clearly, "No, you are not."

I was scared. She sounded like a robot. "Mom, why'd you say that?"

Her face relaxed. "I don't know, honey. I can't explain it." She turned the faucet on and put her wrist under the stream. "I was stumped about the can. Then something came over me, like a pall . . . I couldn't help myself." She released the can from the opener and tossed it into the trash. "Good riddance, bad rubbish, blah blah. Your mother, the worry wart."

"Bye," I said. I heard her mutter calmly to the sink.

Vista de Oro was a half-mile of gradual incline and Webb had a ten-speed he needed to grow into. His torso leaned precariously from side to side as we went up the street. Behind him on my Royce Union one-speed, I was assured the advantage of stable foot access and the force of superior weight on the trip down. Pedaling at high speeds would've threatened his shaky balance; so much for deluxe bikes. I secretly gloated over this when I caught up to him at the fire road.

"If you win," he said, "I'll give you my Saint Christopher." He lifted the chain from inside his sweaty madras shirt. "And if I win, you have to kiss a ro*dent* and let me watch." I resented his whiny accentuation.

My legs a blur, I closed in on aerodynamic triumph. Webb and my Saint Christopher medal coasted harmlessly in my wake. Then I heard him say, "Adios, sucker." I swiveled my neck and he was gone, veering off onto a Vista de Oro tributary. My eyes stung with hot, humiliating wind. This was when I met the parked car.

I don't remember the moment of impact, or flying past the car, or my head striking the pavement. I learned what I could from stories, deduction, and invention, the postscripts of near misses. Webb Harttrick traveled side streets home, too oblivious or ashamed to seek help. He never disclosed which, and I was too mortified to ask. I stayed where I was for some time; my blood congealed on the asphalt. Street sweepers didn't remove the stains, stunted islands that figured in my dreams even after the county repaved. The car I hit was a black Pontiac station wagon belonging to a Girl Scout troop leader. Though she used it to run wifely errands and transport her children, in retrospect I see the car as a hearse. A Oaxacan gardener, on his way home from cropping palm trees, knocked on the door of the house where a troop songfest pealed forth, and said, "This dying child there is, pardon to disturb the pretty voices." My memory would clothe him in a robe, a rustic visionary. One of the scouts offered my name and the leader phoned my parents. Using a collapsed army cot as a stretcher, my father retrieved me. He feared my neck was broken, but it was my skull. Pacing our circular driveway, my mother greeted him: "I knew it was worse than botulism, I knew!" Our pediatrician, Dr. McCallum, was afraid there were blood clots on my brain. Instead of transporting me for X-rays, he spent the night examining my eyes with a flashlight. Pierce, convinced he might have done more on my behalf, begged my parents to let him stay on the floor in a sleeping bag, Babushka in her cage beside him.

I came to the next morning, surrounded by women—friends and neighbors—gently weeping and moaning. They meant well, keeping vigil with my mother, but obliged me to wake to the audience of doom I'd ultimately see as a Greek chorus. The doctor stepped through them. "Do you know who you are?"

"'Course. Phoebe Sandra Dunn."

"Do you know who this is?" He patted his lapels.

Freckled bald head, soapy medicinal smell, stethoscope. "Dr. . . . Callum?"

"Do you know what happened?"

"Adios, sucker. Was going to win the damn race."

"Good for you." He squeezed my hand in nervous blips and dashes, turning to my mother. "She's with us, in Technicolor."

Her neck flushed, my mother knelt by the bed, pushing back my matted hair. "Any other day of the week I'd slap you silly for that kind of language."

Pierce was with her. "Mom, you never slap us silly. You just hit us."

Hugging each other as if their own bones might break, the ladies shuffled out. Their departure expanded my view, and I noticed my father in the corner, squashed into a child-size wicker rocking chair. He looked damaged, folded up, his olive skin a greenish grey. "Dad," I said. "What's the matter with you?"

"I'm sorry, pumpkin." He was crying. "I'm sorry. A good father protects his family."

"Dad's upset," crooned my mother. "He could've hurt you when he moved you. We thought about calling an ambulance." There was a tender contempt in her voice.

"I . . . I wouldn't let them. I'm a lifeguard, Chrissake, I'm trained." He sobbed into his hands. Dr. McCallum cleared his throat and Pierce checked Babushka in her habitat.

"Everything's fine," my mother trilled. "You're fine, so all's well. Isn't it, Martin? Huh, dear?" My father nodded vigorously, his face still covered.

I was confused. My mother bearing up, my father caving in, those women and the doctor in my bedroom—our home was scrambled, turbulent, and my gawky younger brother provided the only stasis, aside from the walls and furniture. A sickening dizziness crawled through me. I vomited on my mother, brother, doctor, and the cage. Pierce screamed, "No, Babushka, bad, bad girl. Oh, hideous."

Shadows rushed around the room. "I refuse to kiss a rodent. Never."

"No one asked you to, Phoebe," said a silhouette of Pierce. "Geez, why don't you sleep a few more days while we clean up this mess?"

From far away, my mother offered to replace the doctor's suit. "Don't mention it," he said. "That's why I buy my rags at J.C. Penney." I blacked out.

❖ ❖ ❖ ❖

Pierce soon lost Babushka, whose legs were frozen by rigor mortis, and he ranted, "My darling, my Babushka. Why did you have to die? Oh, God, I despise you! I want an autopsy!" He carried on until my father got home. Unable to tolerate the sound of Pierce's bereavement, he hauled his son into the dining room. "You will sit at this table and eat what we put before you. You'll take this with some courage, like a man."

Tears spurted from Pierce's eyes onto his plate. If tear ducts were a measure of manliness, my father would have praised my brother as I did then, inside my injured head.

At this juncture, my mother was only half drunk. "You know, Martin, I recall a man who succumbed to weakness. Pitiful, yes, but charming in his way." Her tone was intimate, dreamy, as if we children were no longer present.

"Thank you for that, Sandra. Bear in mind, we're talking about a rat, not a champion show dog."

"Who needs a champion?" my mother said. "Who can tell what people will love?" She spoke right through the constraints of her son and daughter and the table at which we sat, as if she were performing again for the camera, only now my father held it.

"Babushka was exceptional," Pierce lisped with dignity. "She was a champion rat if there ever was one."

Against my father's wishes, our mother chauffeured us to the vet's but stayed in the car, urging us on without her. Pierce and I counted out $9.50 in singles and change to hear Babushka succumbed to pneumonia, the typical cause of death in aging rodents.

"I should have put a cover on her cage," Pierce said, deranged, like a lover. "At night, Phoebe. I should have kept her warmer."

An Inspired Break

As soon as my father had his educational doctorate, he floundered in his study, rearranging books, re-labeling files, and chewing spearmint gum, a vice he turned to industry by fashioning an eleven-foot lanyard from the wrappers. Before long, he matriculated to a special program in Utah; in three years, he'd have another doctorate, this one in psychology. He wanted to quit education to be a marriage counselor. Each of those summers, in what was probably the soberest state of the union, he studied aberrations in human behavior, while his housebound wife studied liquor as the silent mediator of unspoken family strife.

The last August he spent in Provo was the hottest on record back in the San Fernando Valley—days well over one hundred degrees, nights in the eighties, heat that split the heels of feet, parched the insides of noses, and blotched the inner thighs and arms.

One afternoon during that August, my mother drank her third gin and tonic, clear bitter chemistry that matched the glaze it produced in her eyes. She took lengthy swallows, attacking a need I now know was keener than vision, deeper than thirst; then, I simply thought her blue eyes unnerving in their vacancy. Across the room, I felt them on me as I read my latest in a habit of first-love-and-heartbreak books. She flipped her cigarette lighter over and over on the sheen of the end table.

"I'm glad you're a reader, Phoebe," she said, with drawn-out sincerity. "If you read enough, you'll never think any one person has all the answers." Her ensuing laugh was more shrug than merriment. I ignored her and read about a girl who wantonly kissed a boy.

Pierce exploded into the room through the Dutch door, his dog at his ankles. He and Volare had spent some after-lunch hours on their bellies in the cool adobe tree well where Pierce constructed what he called Stink Bug Freeway. Putting lettuce in the miniature lanes and tunnels, he hoped to entice his first commuters, but Volare had an appetite for greens and snapped up the bait whenever Pierce looked the other way.

"Mom, please, PLEASE," he said. "Can we go swimming?" Defeated and cranky, his face shone with sweat; the dog panted, black-spotted tongue askew.

I closed my book. We weren't allowed to swim without adult supervision, and if my mother were true to recent form, within the hour her chin would settle between her lovely collarbones for what she termed an afternoon nap. Her eyes caught guiltily at mine.

"Let's do like we used to," she chanted, springing from the couch the way faith supposedly sprang from the mustard seed charm she wore on her bracelet. "Like before we had the pool. Let's run through the sprinklers." Ice flew from her empty glass to the carpet where a glad Volare crunched it up.

Pierce touched his tongue pensively to his nose. This was not the answer he expected or desired. He was, however, according to my father, a suggestible child.

"Would you," my father had asked him, "stick your head in a lion's mouth if someone told you to?"

"Is the lion cowardly?" Pierce said. "Is it Androcles's lion?"

"What if they asked you to jump off a cliff?" my father persisted.

"How high of a cliff?" Pierce rejoined. "How deep is the water at the bottom?"

Pierce the cliff diver followed my mother, who fussed with the buttons of her yellow romper. She was not then nor was she ever a staggering drunk. When she drank with commitment, there was a deliberate grace in her movements. In my mind's note-taking, I compared her to the women in diaphanous costumes on a television special about sacred dance. My mother, drunk, moved as though she trailed imaginary scarves from her wrists, as though the folds of a filmy gown swirled around her calves and ankles, and the costume might entangle or trip her if she weren't careful.

I might've stayed inside reading my frivolous novel, or gone to the back porch to check the level of my mother's gin bottle, or practiced on the back of my hand the art of kissing. But I chose to slump in a webbed patio chair, my book held convincingly at chest level.

❀ ❀ ❀ ❀

Pierce, who'd been reciting the Pledge of Allegiance as he often did when he was inexplicably nervous, clamped his mouth shut and knelt with his arms around Volare's neck.

We watched our mother draw her long, freckled limbs from her romper, smoothing it flat as paper doll clothes on the brown and white awning that shaded the master bedroom window.

"There," she said, and faced us, a goddess in white undies. She raised the sprinkler key like a scepter and turned the X-shaped valve. "Now we can begin." Her romper cooperatively slid from the awning; funnels of spray burst from the grass. She unwrapped Pierce from Volare and took his hand, strolling into the water and around the lawn's perimeter.

This is unusual, I thought. We'd discussed strange scientific facts at school: two-headed snakes, test tube life, the resilient common cold, the suicide of dolphins. Yet here was a truly baffling phenomenon. Not only was my mother wide awake, in spite of her daytime drinks, but she cavorted about the yard like a flirtatious schoolgirl, in her underclothes, no less. I imagined her carrying a parasol, giggled, then did what any alert observer burdened with proof would do. I went for my camera, a plastic Brownie my father had given me when Kodak came out with the streamline models. I peered down into the black box, my mother arranged her face into the smile she at one time was paid for, Pierce pointed at me self-consciously, and Volare sat up and rolled over. I froze a few moments in shades of grey, which did not do justice to the red-gold of my mother's wet hair in the hot sun, or my brother's prancing instinct to please, or the sound of Volare's lips scooping droplets from the air.

Then I resumed my reading.

❀ ❀ ❀ ❀

For privacy, the houses in our neighborhood had Masonite slats woven through their chain-link fences; from above, these must have resembled a continuous protective membrane between clustered cells. If you wanted to spy, you couldn't be nonchalant about it: you had to purposely climb and gaze boldly into someone else's backyard. Laird Benwell, our next-door-neighbor, mounted the ladder beside his yacht, the *Edith Marie,* named for his wife well before its completion, and stared down at us.

There was a joke among my mother's woman friends that Benwell's yacht got to be oversized and took him so long to construct because he wanted an excuse to spy on my mother when she potted daisies or lay in the sun, and that he named it after his wife to appease her jealousy.

I disliked Benwell for a number of reasons, not the least of which was that he'd dumped Tokyo Rose, his family's pet, at the Humane Society. He claimed the monkey was the cause of his sons' perennial colds, but he'd actually got rid of her shortly after she escaped her cage and hung upside-down from our roof, in front of the kitchen window. My mother, doing the dishes, had run screaming into the front drive, flailing her scrub cloth like a flag of distress.

"Hey, Sandy," he yelled now from over the fence. He was the only person I knew who imposed a nickname on my mother. She and Pierce tossed a tennis ball in a soggy game of keep-away from the dog. Volare twirled and snapped at the challenge, his black curls whipping more spray into the air; Pierce laughed rapid fire at the dog's acrobatics; the sprinklers hissed. My mother couldn't have heard Laird Benwell if she'd wanted to.

He resorted to me. "Some heat wave we're having, eh Feebah-reebah?"

"Yeah, Mr. Benwell," I said. "Pretty hot, all right."

"Oops," he said, wagging his hammer at me. "Remember? It's *Doctor* Benwell." He was a chiropractor, about whom my father said, "The man's not an MD, and I won't have my children spouting his lies." So, we had license to be taciturn, though not overtly rude, with Benwell and his admonitions.

I tipped my book and nodded at Mr. Benwell.

"Looks like your mom's found a way to beat the weather." He regarded her with an eager expression he'd never worn before today, which induced me to take another glance at my mother.

She was fairly well soaked from the sprinklers by now, her pageboy sleek to her head as a seal's pelt. The cones of her bra collapsed into the circles of their stitching, and her nylon underpants clung like opaque sandwich wrap. Wisps and curls of pubic hair formed a relief map that I guessed intrigued Benwell, and his probable interest made me feel both protective and ashamed of my mother. She and Pierce hung by their hands from a tree limb, poking their toes at the leaping dog.

I picked up my camera and snapped a picture of Benwell, gargoyle leering above the fine spray. He began to pound nails intently. I photographed my mother and brother, kicking in midair. I turned and shot my mother's yellow romper, bunched like a cake decoration on the dull concrete patio. I made sure Benwell was still hammering before I went into the house.

❀ ❀ ❀ ❀

Though we lived in what was left of a citrus orchard, freshly squeezed juice was a rarity. Most of the neighborhood found its Vitamin C in pills or canned concentrate. My mother would soon be wanting more to drink, more glaze for her disquieting eyes. I believed I could coerce her into having an alternative to a tall gin and tonic if I mixed a drink as complicated and enticing as the one she'd habitually taken to. Thus I set about preparing lemonade from scratch.

I stretched my T-shirt into a hammock for a dozen lemons from our tree out front, then mashed them in an old leaded juicer that resembled a manual water pump. To the pitcher of juice, I added water and a small hill of sugar, but a sip of it was intolerably sour. After additional mounds of sugar, it remained sour. I heard the house pipes shudder as the sprinklers went off. My mother, toweling herself and Pierce dry, would be in momentarily, rummaging the refrigerator and cabinets for the ingredients of her cocktail. (My mother was not only graceful in her carriage as a drunk, she was also meticulous about stowing her accoutrements, as if she expected each drink to be final.) Rushed, I poured a bottle of carbonated lemon-lime into the pitcher, loaded tumblers with ice cubes, and suspended maraschino cherries on miniature plastic swords across the rims.

In the hall closet, I dug out appliquéd napkins, wedding gifts my mother never used. ("I had such plans," she said. "Plans for elegant afternoon teas. Then I realized if I invited anyone to a tea party, they'd think I was in line for the loony bin." The Dutch door, too, was a remnant of my mother's planning, her touch to the house when it was built. With such a door, she told me, "You can shut out the unacceptable part of the world and welcome in the part you want.") I folded the napkins into triangles and fanned them out on a lacquered rattan serving tray, adding the pitcher, tumblers, and a bowl of extra cherries. This was a beautiful, unwieldy load. I balanced it carefully.

The Dutch door slammed, vibrating the picture windows. Pierce yelled, "Phoebe! Phoebe, guess what? Volare just burped, louder and better than any human!" He crashed head-on into me as he rounded a corner. For a moment, the tray stayed wedged between our torsos, then we backed away, the wind knocked out of us, and my careful arrangement dropped.

Nothing broke, all plastic and bamboo for poolside use. There wasn't the drama of shattered glass and blood. Waiting for my breath and Pierce's apology, I stared at the foaming soup on the linoleum. The cherries bobbed, sailing across the floor until the spillage leveled out. Pierce lost his breath as soon as he regained it, laughing hysterically.

"Oh, yes!" he spat through his lisp. "Classic pileup. Do you think we cracked any ribs?"

His laughter incensed me. My plans for reforming my mother lay spoiled at his feet, along with her favorite white napkins, now pink. How could this salivating, gap-toothed organism find joy in a mishap of such sad and wasteful proportion? I grabbed him by the shoulders and shoved him to his knees.

"Lick it," I said. "Lick it up like the dog you are."

Without moving his head, Pierce lifted his large eyes to make sure I wasn't joking. I wasn't. He lapped at the floor, and I continued to berate him as if he were responsible for what was wrong with our family, including and especially my inability to change whatever that was.

My mother, sylphlike when under the influence, had sneaked into the house and stood in the hallway watching us, waiting for understanding to hit her. Instead, a reluctant horror developed in the set of her jaw and brow. I thought she was horrified at the ruin of her napkins until she bent down to Pierce.

"You don't have to do that, honey," she said, coaxing him up from under his chin. "Not for anyone in the world, not even Phoebe."

Then she grabbed my pigtail with her right hand, the pressure point of my elbow with her left, and pushed me into her back porch, her domain. She shut the door, about to say what was unfit for Pierce's radar ears. Turning me at the waist, she backed me up against the counter and the neatly piled tubs of folded clothes.

"Tell me," she said, and shook me. "When did you get so mean? When did you turn into a nasty old lady?"

"When did you revert to childhood and become the play-

mate of your nine-year-old son?" I crossed my arms and jut-
ted my chin.

She slapped me hard on the side of my face, where I could
tell she intended to inflict pain as well as punishment. And
she sobbed, opened a cabinet, searching the soaps and pol-
ishes for the bottle that had begun to mean as much to her as
a tidy house.

I helped Pierce mop up. "Sorry," he said, sheepishly.

"Me too," I said. "But the lemonade took eons to make,
and I wanted us to have it together."

He passed me a salvaged cherry on a sword; I ate it.
"You're still my sister," he said, "even when you're a nightmare
to behold."

Out back, I retrieved my mother's romper. From his ladder perch, Laird Benwell hollered, "Hey, Feeb, no more water sports today?" He smoothed back his greasy hair. Volare
yawned from the flattened patch of ivy geraniums where he
rested coolly.

"Right, Mr. Benwell. No more for today." I waved him off
as I leaned into the Dutch door.

Already, my mother was asleep, her underwear printing a
dark gold outline of her on the buff-colored couch. The sprinklers had been a side trip, an inspired break, and now she was
back to her routine, an hour later than usual. I folded her
outfit and put it gently in her lap. I took my camera from the
windowsill. The late afternoon light glistened on the barely
touched drink on the coffee table in front of her, and I made
sure I had that in the picture.

❀❀❀❀

Before my father returned from Utah for a weekend visit, I
organized and labeled the photographs. "Point your toes," I
wrote on one; "Dr. Voyeur," on another; "Nap Time," on the
last in the sequence. I put the photos in an invitingly plain
envelope, which I buried in his stack of mail. As he leafed
through it, I positioned myself in the hallway. He came to my
envelope, paused, and opened it slowly. He tilted the pictures

away from and toward the mullioned window, hoping he'd find a trick of light or perspective.

Any time my father was confused or disbelieving, his eyes bulged like globes and his irises reflected grey in patches, accenting the darker areas. These shapes reminded me of continents yet to be discovered or explored.

"Christ on a crutch, Sandra," he said, and struggled to focus, to recognize, evaluate. "Laird Benwell, of all people. Did you have to pick a chiropractor as the witness for your exhibition?"

In my room, I doubled the pillow behind my neck and read. The girl broke up with the boy she'd so eagerly kissed. She of course felt terrible about it; the boy begged her to tell him how he might change, but her resolve didn't falter at his distress. She'd pledged herself to the preservation of ruins the world over—Tulum, Stonehenge, Athens, Giza—and couldn't be responsible for someone who'd follow and want to kiss her in the shadows of a civilization's triumph and decay. My critical side dismissed the girl as rather full of herself and disloyal, though I knew my mother would applaud her unerring ambition.

QUEEN OF THE TREE OF THE DEAD

THE YEAR I DEVELOPED BREASTS, a tree died in our front yard. The events, of course, were gradual and unrelated; memory has fixed them and made them companionable. The sick tree was a grapefruit Pierce and I climbed and nailed boards on, though we never finished a legitimate fort.

When I heard the tree was diseased, I was taken aback. I remembered the nauseating pain in my head after my skull was fractured, pain that for two weeks prevented my hair from being brushed. I remembered, too, how shocked I was to learn that bone registered pain, that bone was more than an impervious framework for holding upright and separate all other body parts capable of hurting. I thought with chagrin of the tree's limbs and branches on which we'd happily hammered, stomped, bounced, and swung. I wondered if, somehow, my brother and I had broken the tree's will to live.

The first outward symptom was when the tree dropped leaves in clumps, as if invisible fingers that held them in place all at once gave up and let go. My mother gathered the leaves in grocery bags, and my father sawed off the bare branches. "Probably just suckers," he said. "It'll thrive now without them."

But the tree developed a more troubling symptom: fissures opened in its trunk and limbs, and from them oozed a substance the color of honey and the texture of tar. Once, I tried to taste the amber sap but couldn't transfer it from my finger to my tongue. A whiff of the resin told me I wasn't missing much. Still, there was a golden, gem-like quality about the tree's wounds that drew me to them and repelled me at the same time. How could the hardness of wood and bone know pain? How could a tree be both seriously ill and beautiful in the secretions of its illness?

My mother said the tree's wounds wept, while my father said they bled. "We've got an upper branch bleeding," my father said. "Have to get out there this weekend."

"I keep thinking," my mother said, "we should just be able to bandage where it weeps and make it better."

Despite their disparate terminologies, my parents united in trying to save the tree. My mother chose leaf and branch tending over drinking, and my father spent less time alone in his den. Both called the tree's disease *Gaposis*. I never learned whether that was the correct botanical term or if they coined it in their rare state of collusion.

While ministering to the tree, my father's responsibility was to saw off all infected limbs, cut them into fireplace-size bits, and cart them in a wheelbarrow to the wood-yard. My mother then mixed a baby blue paint, chalky as stomach medications (Pierce and I called it "Pepto Bismol for Plantlife"), and brushed it onto the circle of newly exposed wood. Our parents worked well together, almost single-mindedly, and occasionally exchanged duties, my mother pushing the wheelbarrow, my father concocting the paint. Initially, tree doctoring was a once-a-month job, but it escalated to an every weekend affair until finally the tree was a skeleton of stunted limbs marked by large blue dots that reminded me of what blurred my vision when my mother hired a professional photographer to do our family portraits.

Besides being attractively strange, the dead tree was eminently climbable, free of stickery twigs and bee-covered blossoms. It had perches, top to bottom, with sure handholds and footholds, and the barren tree became a neighborhood jungle gym. Most school-day afternoons, it held at least a couple of children in its lopped-off limbs, even when Pierce and I studied indoors.

My mother took a snapshot of the tree one afternoon when several of us crowded its perches, because, she said, it made her glad to see the casualty serve some purpose after death. On the lowest branch sat Tina Spitz, daughter of the disreputable plate glass salesman next door on the right. Since her father's brief jail term, she'd been sent to public school and beleaguered by taunters who followed her home and called her "Tina Transvestite." No one clearly understood the reasons for the slur, except that, whether she wore a skirt or trousers, Tina never seemed comfortable in her own skin, having grown up in a house where only the peacocks strutted behind the locked gate with their heads held high. The rest of us in the tree weren't brave enough to overtly defend her, though we didn't join the name calling, and we let her, slouched and eyes downcast, walk home safely on the fringes of our group.

On counterpoised limbs were Carlton and Ramon Benwell, rid at last of their chiropractor father's garlic necklaces, now brandishing a ball peen hammer each. They used the implements to smash sow bugs they rolled into balls and lined up by twenties and thirties along the curb. They had a stopwatch and competed for speed and accuracy in smashing. Pierce would occasionally keep time for them, his back turned on the proceedings. He straddled a branch just below me, clutching his desiccated coonskin cap and a transistor radio. The radio was on full volume, and I had threatened to drool on it if he didn't turn it down and stop singing "Society's Child" in a fake falsetto, drowning out the plaintive voice of the singer. The hem of the white cotton T-shirt I wore barely met the waistband of my pants, and I indignantly pulled at it when Pierce said he could look through and see all the way up to my chin.

In the topmost crook of the tree crouched Dessa Hauser, the oldest of our entourage and my best friend. On her mane of wavy hair, she sported a rhinestone tiara, a relic of her mother's, who years before had been UCLA's Tropicana Queen and now displayed the keepsake on a velvet pillow atop the Hausers' baby grand. Whenever Dessa could, she smuggled the tiara out of the house, and we played a game we called "Queen of the Tree of the Dead." It was a morbid combination of Simon Says and Statue Maker, wherein Dessa, the Queen, gave a command to start, and we writhed on our respective branches and moaned as though we were the most disconsolate, tortured zombies and ghouls ever condemned to wander the earth. When she told us to stop, we had to freeze in the contortion she caught us in. Whoever laughed, coughed, or lost balance had to find a four-leaf clover or a cocoon before resuming position in the tree.

Dessa dispatched us into action just as my mother framed her shot. "You kids are just adorable," she said, shaking back her hair and the invisible scarves of her liquor. "You look like little monkeys and birds on the tree of life."

So misguided was my mother's perception that even woe-ful Tina Spitz cracked a grin for the camera.

A few weeks later at the dinner table, my mother passed the photo to my father. "Martin, our firstborn needs a train-ing bra," she chirped. "Phoebe's little breasts stick out like nobody's business."

My father shyly said, "Hmmm, you're right."

Pierce sprayed milk through his nose, valiantly attempt-ing to avoid laughter. When he recovered, he belched and said, "I knew that without a picture."

❀ ❀ ❀ ❀

The tree stood, leafless, as long as we lived in the house. For a short while, it incited controversy. Laird Benwell complained the tree was an attractive nuisance; my father reminded Ben-well of the yacht that had been taking shape in his yard for over a decade and was still nowhere near completion. Ben-well backed down. Then Harold Spitz sent a letter alluding to property value, which my father answered with a note alluding to zoning and exotic pets, wondering if peacocks were classi-fied as such. Spitz did not reply. So my father, who disliked ad-mitting defeat nearly as much as he disliked failure itself, kept the dead tree standing in defiance of neighborhood opinion.

Badness Is a Calling

For my parents, dinnertime became an elaborate dance of avoidance. Delivering bowls to the table, my mother spun like radar attuned to and repelled by the echoes of my father's pulse. My father parried like a spy satellite, orbiting her at a guarded distance. They sat beside each other, passing food to us, and didn't so much as brush arm hairs.

My father, his brief principalship behind him, was in practice full-time and regaled us with case histories at the table: a man who preferred sleeping in his convertible Cadillac under the stars to sleeping in a bed with his wife; a woman who, on a trip to England, had fallen in love with a young actor's performance as Prince Hamlet (she stressed the word *performance*) and whose husband now wanted to take her back to Stratford and murder the fellow; a couple who wondered if it was normal for their six-year-old to fold newspaper boats and set them on fire as he sat amid them in the bathtub; and many complaints involving lawnmowers, electric shavers, and portable hairdryers used at odd hours. My father never violated his code of ethics by revealing names. If he updated us on a case, he'd say, "Young pyromaniac has graduated to lighting rolls of toilet paper," or "Stratford-on-Avon is willing to forget if her husband will forgive."

My father seemed more than mildly interested in our re-actions to his tales of peculiarity. I saw him mentally weighing our strangeness against the strangeness of others as he took us all in—Pierce, me, my mother last.

My mother built a repertoire of responses to my father's mealtime stories. She examined the tines of her fork; burned holes in the tablecloth with inch-long cigarette ashes; crossed her eyes at us when our father wasn't looking; got up from the table to freshen her drink; chipped or cracked, but never shattered, several blue onion plates in a set of sixteen; hummed romantic songs like "Fly Me to the Moon" or "Some Enchanted Evening" while my father spoke; stared at her reflection in the kitchen window, her chin cupped in her hands in an attitude of rapt boredom; pushed my bangs off my face and threatened to trim them right there at the table; ran her hands through her thick hair and talked of needing a frost job.

After dinner, my father returned to his den and spoke into a tape recorder, confidently unraveling the threads of his cases.

When Pierce and I shut off the TV and delivered ourselves to our rooms, we sometimes heard violent whispers from within the master bedroom. This was how our parents fought.

"That's eerie," Pierce said. "Why can't they yell at each other out in the open?"

"Because," I said, "then we could yell at them to stop and they might have to obey their children. How embarrassing."

❀ ❀ ❀ ❀

Unlike evil, which is its own cold source, badness is a calling, a passion. Odessa Hauser had been summoned, and I'd loved her unreservedly since she was five and I was close behind her. We met, her green eye peering at my brown, between the slats woven through the chain-link fence. She lived one street over; our yards backed into each other.

"Get off my property," she said.

"You get off mine," I said. She threw a handful of dirt against her side of the fence, and I splatted my side with a rotten orange. Next, she invited me over to help exterminate gophers, which required one person putting a garden hose down a burrow and the other turning on the water full pressure. Twice, she turned it on before I was ready, and the bucking nozzle bruised my shins.

While my mother told me Santa Claus was a spirit I could believe in as long as I chose to, Dessa said, "Santa is an army of fat old men who can't get jobs any other time of the year. If you want to believe in that, be my guest." While my mother explained the sex act as a man and woman kissing to transfer a seed of love that grew a child, Dessa drew me anatomically correct diagrams that were pictorial satire of my mother's words. While both my parents assured me no one in our neighborhood had ever divorced (I sensed it was a disease easily spread), my friend revealed that her mother, shortly after giving birth, left Dessa's biological father, and Otto Hauser swiftly adopted her. Everyone thought it best not to saddle Dessa with too many authority figures.

"I ask you," she said. "Do I seem like someone who'd confuse a real father with a fake one, or vice versa?" I had to admit, she was not a likely candidate for such confusion. Her mind was a warm-blooded polygraph test. She called him "Daddy" to his face and "Daddy Otto" at all other times.

Pierce might have adored Dessa as I did, but she, an only child, couldn't appreciate the paradox of being a sibling, of knowing affection and loathing in equal measures. Within Pierce's hearing, she said, "How can you stand that lint ball, clinging to you all the time? What's with his dog's tongue—leprosy? Syphilis?" As Pierce grew older and his attachment to Volare deepened, he protected his dog from her blasphemy by avoiding us.

My parents kept their fights from Pierce and me the way Dessa Hauser's parents kept naked pictures of each other in their bureau drawers. Dessa brought the photographs to homeroom one day and passed them to everyone except the teacher, while Dessa's parents continued to believe in their privacy.

I waited for the fascination over Dessa's photographs to subside at Amerigo Vespucci Junior High. When groups of deliciously aghast girls no longer danced circles around my friend, I approached her with concerns over my parents. What ailed them? Why didn't they fume and shout and take shocking pictures of each other afterward when they reconciled? I'd checked every drawer in their bedroom and found nothing but a rubber-banded stack of flowery anniversary cards.

During the noise of nutrition break, Dessa quietly pondered my questions, pulling and gnawing at the coil of her cinnamon roll. Finished, she said, "Your dad's just started to rake in the money. Give it time. Has your mom ever redecorated?"

I said the house had been virtually the same since I'd lived there, old furniture and carpet either reupholstered or replaced in kind.

"You wait, Phoebe, pretty soon your mom'll redecorate. My mother says redecoration holds more marriages together than outside help, no offense meant to your father. She says there are women in the neighborhood who change their living rooms every year, and they're the ones with the biggest smiles at the supermarket."

"No chance, romance," I said, and meant it. I couldn't imagine my mother, the uncommonly smooth drinker, tripped by so shallow a rut. But in March, on my birthday, I came home from school to a Bedrosian Interiors truck in our driveway, and a room-size Dumpster parked along the curb. Pierce sat forlornly on the front lawn, twirling Volare's neck curls. Two swarthy young men, one with raging acne, lugged a lopsided cylinder of braided carpet and hoisted it into the trash container. I tossed my binder and math book next to my brother.

"They're ripping up the house, Phoebe," Pierce said. "Gutting it like a beautiful rainbow trout." He'd recently embarked on a failure of a campout with my father, during which Pierce became physically ill over what followed the excitement of the catch. My father, who'd bought Pierce a hunting knife for the occasion, said, "Son, you'll have to give that back if you're not willing to use it." Pierce handed it over, no protest.

The worker with acne reemerged with my desk top, a solid oak door my father had fixed for me across two of his smaller file cabinets. While seated at the makeshift desk, I did homework, read, and lay my head on the wood, which had the familiar smell of an old blanket and was stained, like shoe leather and wristwatch bands, with the oils of my skin. I would think about and beyond what I read. If, for example, there were anti-matter and anti-worlds, what would the antithesis of Phoebe Dunn be? Would she have light hair instead of dark, curly and fine instead of thick and straight? Would she be cheerful instead of pensive? Would she be a he? Just how far did the anti-concept extend? When I exhausted a line of thought, I carved, with a nail file, cryptic messages mixed with song lyrics: *Help*, and *The children are cool*, and *I've gotta get out of this place*, and *I got troubles, worries, wounds to bind.* The gouged oak grain was my concession to diary keeping. Now a stranger with a blue battleground of a face carried my desk as though it were a junked surfboard.

"Excuse me," I said, touching him on the arm. "That's my desk. Please don't throw it away."

He sniggered, teeth flashing white against his painful skin color. "Talk to your mother, okay, little Susie? I'm just doing a job." He raised the door to the lip of the Dumpster.

I pulled the hem of his yellowed T-shirt. "I said, *don't.*"

"Hey." He slapped behind himself at me and pushed the door over the rim, which vibrated as the load hit bottom. "You don't touch me, girl, little prissy lady-girl. You don't own me, you don't own my uncle's business, you don't own nothing. You don't even know the difference between a desk and a stinking door." He verged on righteous tears. I left him stammering under Pierce's gaze, which wavered between confusion and curiosity.

Inside, my mother put her drink on the kitchen counter and took my hand. "Come on, Phoebe, come look." She led me down the exposed concrete hallway to my room. "You're a real student, so here's a real desk." Boxy, antique white with gold leaf trim, shiny brass drawer handles and a matching swivel chair—it looked like a vanity table, a place for preening rather than work.

"Happy birthday, honey," my mother said. "Happy fourteenth."

With difficulty, I thanked her, locked myself in the bathroom, and started to cry. My real desk rested at the bottom of a rapidly filling trash bin destined for the city dump. I wept that I wasn't strong or bold enough to retrieve the door, nor was I sufficiently angry to generate the adrenaline that might have given me strength to act. I thought of news articles about people who lifted automobiles by themselves, freeing trapped victims; people who, without considering the consequences, dashed into burning buildings to save squalling infants. I couldn't summon such resolve. Miserable, I pondered my face in the bathroom mirror until I grew sick of watching my lips quiver and my eyes leak. I rinsed my face, dried it with a towel redolent of fabric softener. In my reflection, I saw my mother's sad and stupidly hopeful face combined with my father's dark coloring and pragmatic brow. Mr. Bedrosian's nephew outside was right: I owned nothing. At the moment, I could distinguish no vestige of myself from the features of the two who made me.

"Are you all right?" my mother asked, though she clearly had her answer. "What's wrong? Tell me."

"I'm fine," I snapped. "Leave me alone."

Leave me alone was the first message I carved in the bland finish of the new desk. I used the tip of an inkless fountain pen, hummed my favorite songs, and made sure the carving was too deep for lemon oil to cure. I covered the message with the blotter my mother had placed on the desk for protection.

Pierce wasn't as daunted as I was by the huge Dumpster. He discovered his Roy Rogers hat stand missing and stomped outside, clambering into the bin, where he completely disappeared from my view on the brick entry porch. Volare barked as pieces of plasterboard, plywood, carpet, and padding rose and fell, and finally out came the projectile hat stand, studded with its stirrups, spurs, and saddle horns. Pierce followed, boosting himself up and over the container's edge. He carried the stand like a lance back into the house and set it decisively in its assigned corner of his room.

When the hat stand disappeared again, the Dumpster was brim full. Pierce, agile as a rat, scrambled over the debris, alert for a telltale glint of spur. I scrambled with him; before, I'd thought the hat stand juvenile and silly—who wore hats except Pierce?—but it, unlike my desk top, was portable enough to be retrieved, and retrieval was the urgent issue.

"This is outrageous," Pierce said, tugging at a shower curtain embossed with tropical fish. "I practically grew up with that hat stand, and it doesn't take up much floor space."

I shook my head in sympathetic bewilderment, and pried open an old patio umbrella that enfolded the hat stand.

"Nice save, sister," he said. He took the stand to the garage, where he locked it to his bicycle with a chain. Both items, which Pierce once treasured, remained bound together in disuse until they were sold separately at a yard sale.

That night, as emissary to my father, I knocked on the door of his study. "Dad, it's me."

"Family interruption," he said into the recording machine. It clicked off as he called my name.

I sat on his braided carpet—the only piece my mother hadn't scrapped—and moved my palms over its lumps and loose ends. I asked him what he thought of the house's transformation-in-progress and the upheaval it had caused.

"Your mother's department, not mine," he said and gave me a feeble grin.

I fisted my hands. "Doesn't anyone else have a right to comment? We live here too."

"Phoebe, why are you so tough on your mother? Sandra is doing her thing." He struck a note of apology for using the already tired expression. "If she weren't doing it, she'd be terribly bored." He glanced furtively at his tape recorder.

"Oh, boredom," I said, rising to my feet. "So that's what you call it. I've been trying to put a finger on her problem."

❀ ❀ ❀

Late June and early July, my father camped in his den, fed Volare, ate his meals out, rinsed off in the swimming pool, and shaved at his office. The rest of us abandoned the house while the kitchen and bathrooms were unusable, and stayed at

Laguna Beach in a mildewed apartment complex that sagged on the cliff of an exquisite cove. During her send-off, Dessa crooned, "You're going to meet a guy, I know it." I rolled my eyes, unable to think beyond the impending torment of three weeks in close, damp quarters in the company of my mother without her back porch and Pierce without his dog.

Copa de oro and bougainvillea vines seemed to hold Crescent Bay Terrace together, tenuously attach it to the cliff, hide and beautify its numerous structural imperfections with gold and magenta blooms. Upon arrival, I loathed the place, its shoddiness, creakiness, and musty odors. I snapped on my lipstick pink two-piece and parked myself and my book on a towel in the hot sand, pretending, as best I could, I didn't know my mother or Pierce when they traipsed down the slate steps. Seated behind my mother, I counted how many cigarettes she smoked and stuck in the sand beside her. I went for walks and, with force that bordered on cruelty, poked my toes in sea anemones in tide pools. I bobbed in the salty water until my fingers were mushy.

Suddenly, though, the apartment house became charming as a Mediterranean villa: my mother a tragically unfulfilled woman, the tide pools homes of mysterious ocean life, the sea itself a larger mystery.

His name was Todd. He was eighteen, from Bakersfield. He came to Laguna with his family, and he would enter basic training at Camp Pendleton after the vacation. Todd had straight, shiny black hair, black eyes, and the full mouth of a girl. He wore his red swim trunks slung low on his narrow hipbones, and followed me on one of my walks.

"My mom told me you were only fourteen years old," he said, switching a kelp branch against my leg. "I couldn't believe it. You act much older."

"Huh, really?" I hoped he couldn't see my heart thudding behind my stretchy bathing suit.

"Yeah, almost conceited, like a snooty college girl. Nose in the air or in a book, one or the other."

"Right, that's me, a regular coed." I snatched the kelp from him and with nervous energy began to pop the bulbs of fruit.

He joined me, and we assaulted more of the bulbs, laughing when they popped, as if each struck a different and more surprising note. He dragged a new branch up from the shoreline foam, and we burst every bulb on that one, too.

In the next two weeks, Todd and I went for long afternoon swims, Australian crawling past the breakers and halfway to the seal rocks. We arfed at the seals, floated on our backs, had contests to see who could spew water the farthest. My head ached, some of those days, from the amount of salt I swallowed or absorbed through the spongy lining of my inner mouth.

"That Todd is certainly a cute one," my mother loudly remarked one evening after I stepped out of the shower. I could feel and hear her expectant waiting outside the warped bathroom door. "He's taken with you, Phoebe. You're a young woman now."

I cringed. The last time she'd made this pronouncement on behalf of my womanhood was at the dinner table the day I began menstruating. Then and now, I silently mused what I should say in reply: Thank you? Yes, I am? No, not quite, not yet?

"You're not doing anything your father and I would be ashamed of, are you?"

"My gosh, Mother," I said, whipping past her in my towel. "You won't let me stay out after dark. Plus he's much too old for me, and he's going to war."

"That's precisely my point," she said.

In the courtyard of the Terrace was a pay phone on which she talked to my father after I was in bed. The ugly, embarrassing word *oversexed* wafted up to my window, and I wasn't sure whether she used it in reference to me or the boy I loved because he was there and willing. Either way, I resented her intrusive concern and guessed it was prompted by jealousy: I had something other than the contents of an expensive gin bottle to transport me.

❋ ❋ ❋

The day before my family left Laguna, Todd and I went for a final swim. Both of us were quiet and glum, staring out at the rocks we had swum toward and barked at, unsure how to say goodbye. His foot brushed between my legs, which startled me, and I thought it an accident, but he did it again, and then again, and then with a rhythm like the rocking of the water. I turned to him, my eyes round with questions.

"Please," he said, drawing closer. "I might be dead by Christmas. Please let me enjoy this day with the most beautiful girl on the beach."

I was also the only female over ten and under thirty on the beach, but his breath, warmer than the air, tingled on the nape of my neck. "Please," he said. "I want to kiss you, but I can't tell if your mom is watching through her sunglasses." I pictured her sad, freckled gaze behind me as I took in the shimmering horizon and was reminded of when I looked into one of two mirrors opposite each other, how blurry the reflections became when they took off for infinity.

"Please," Todd said, and his foot or the saltwater made me wonderfully buoyant. The curve where his leg met his foot bounced me like a bicycle seat. "You just look like you're treading water, or like a sea horse. Don't be nervous. Please, don't be." I knew he was trying to comfort himself as well as me, so I rose high, and higher, and sank in prismatic underwater light where we awkwardly bumped against each other like seals on land. A current went through me that seemed to alternate the warmth of the air and the cool of the ocean. I must have looked frightened when I broke the water's surface; Todd asked if I'd ever had the feeling before. I said no, though I wasn't sure whether he meant love or the physical jolts that originated in my crotch and pulsed, with my heart, to my extremities.

Todd wrote me a letter from Pendleton. He called me a great girl and the smartest sea horse ever. I mailed him a scented note card in which I confessed my love for him, and which, in retrospect, makes my eyes burn at such idealism and trust. There was no other mail from him, and I hoped for years he had another girl in Bakersfield, or had met one in Nam, and that he made it back with every shiny hair on his head intact.

❋ ❋ ❋ ❋

"Don't tell me," Dessa said, home from her vacation just in time for school. She stood on our brick steps, her hands over her eyes. "I knew it'd be you before me. Did he kiss you?"

"No," I said. I didn't yet have the reserve of sexual experience to explain the day in the water, that what had happened was more athletic than a kiss but less painful than what we'd heard about going all the way.

"Take me on the tour, then," she murmured, relieved, parting her hands like a theatre curtain. "Surprise me with rich reds and deep blues, leather, velvet, corduroy."

"I wish," I said. "Then you wouldn't need blinders to watch TV in here. You don't have to be quiet—she's snoring." Her project complete, my mother had resumed the afternoon naps.

Dessa stared. She chewed a segment of her auburn hair, sniffed it, and poked it against her cheek as if testing her senses.

My mother had effected as dire a change as possible, short of razing the house: the living room, bedrooms, and hallways were carpeted in off-white shag and protected with a complex trail of plastic runners; the living room's Western red cedar walls, beams, mantelpiece, and cathedral ceiling were painted off-white, as were the bricks of the hearth; the kitchen's rooster print wallpaper was removed and replaced with off-white, burlap-textured paper that had marble-like veins of metallic gold throughout; tiles laid on the kitchen counter and floor matched the wallpaper; tiles flecked with brown and beige were laid in the bathrooms (*Fly feces,* Pierce and I remarked. *Insect outhouses.*); the buff-colored couch and wing chairs were upholstered in off-white hopsacking; the cedar window seats, sills, bookshelves, closet doors, dressers, headboards, nightstands—all vestiges of wood were enameled in off-white. She kept the dining room table the same, calico and maple, though they were pitifully out of place in the altered scheme.

Dessa squirmed at both knowing and not recognizing where she was. "This is so white," she said, "it could start a race riot."

"It's so white," I returned, "I feel like I'm in one of her cream sauce casseroles."

My mother rolled over, sounding the box springs in her open bedroom. "Not white," she shouted. "Ivory! Pearl!"

"Oops," Dessa said. We giggled into a silence Pierce interrupted with a conspiratorial whisper.

"This is white as paper," he said. "White as paper you're supposed to write on."

A playfulness that had been absent from them for months came into his eyes. With the redecoration of the house and the hat stand incident, Pierce ceased his spontaneous marches, songs, recitations, dirt sculpting, and threw himself into one of two activities: reading about American Indian tribal rites, or clutching his Fender electric as he listened to a transistor radio. When he especially liked the music—"You're Pushin' Too Hard" by the Seeds was a favorite—he strummed the muted strings of the guitar. By our father's decree, Pierce could use the amplifier for two afternoon hours on Saturday, one on Sunday.

Volare was consigned to the back, a "yard dog" at my mother's orders. She didn't want the tufts of black hair the dog would leave on the carpet or on the sides of the couch, chair, or bedspread he'd surely rub up against. Pierce, instead of spending more time outdoors with Volare, practically deserted him. Each picture window was smudged with the pleadings of Volare's muzzle. The dog, now seeing Pierce, pressed the fleur-de-lis of his nose against the pane, and fluttered his growl in something like a tune.

Pierce stealthily closed my mother's door so he could let Volare in without her waking. "Here," he said, bending to remove the dog's collar. "So you don't make that jingling." The dog slunk around the room, naked without the weight and noise he associated with movement, confused by the new indoor aromas.

Pierce planted himself in front of Dessa. "I know you're not extra fond of me," he said. "But would you mind holding on to this?" He slipped the collar over her arm.

Dessa's smallish, sloppily painted mouth pursed into a trace of frosty pink. She was guarded, studying Pierce's odd behavior; maybe her accomplished badness caught scent of the incipient. I'd never seen Pierce stride until that afternoon.

Before, his natural gait was as close to scuttling as that of any biped I'd encountered.

He strode into my father's study.

He came out with his confiscated hunting knife.

"Exhibit A," he said, unsheathing the blade.

Dessa and I slowly faced each other, drawing breath, exchanging perplexed glances to excuse ourselves from intervening. We absolutely wanted to see what Pierce had in mind. I tried to calm the skittish dog by patting his rump, and he, unaccustomed to the plastic runners, slid into prone position, legs splayed front and rear.

"Don't anyone worry," Pierce said. "I've planned this all out."

He sliced the flesh at the tip of his left thumb, a good clean cut, no flinching. "Indians did this for ceremony and so can I. Blood is sacred and meaningful." His voice sounded different to me, though it hadn't yet started to be crackly or lower.

Pierce squeezed his thumb like a tube of ointment, and in his loopy backhand script spelled his given name on the carpet beneath the coffee table. He drew a heart next to his writing, sliced his index finger, and bled his name and a swastika in the space between the couch and a pole lamp. "This symbol was used for healing long before it came to mean hate," he said. He lifted the couch cushions and left a circle of droplets under each, carefully reassembling the couch with his bloodless hand. All of this he did with the authority of a magician.

Then he said, "Dessa can put the collar back on the dog," which she did without pause. Volare whined for escape at the Dutch door and she let him out.

"Unreal," Dessa said, chewing her hair again.

"Yes, it was," Pierce said, smiling widely through his braces.

I made him wash his hands with disinfectant and realized what had changed about his voice.

His lisp was gone.

❀ ❀ ❀ ❀

My mother discovered Pierce's mischief after it dried and set.

She gasped, blinked rapidly, and fell to her knees for a closer inspection. "Oh my poor baby," she said. Not a word more until my father came home from work. That night, my parents held a marathon that tried the limits of whispering and concluded with my mother's imploded sobs, the bedroom door sucking open, and the clink of ice cubes in a glass.

My father beckoned us to his den. "Why, son?" he said, his eyes widening to reveal those mysterious continents. "Why graffiti on the expensive floor, and with something you have to know is indelible?"

"I felt like it," Pierce said, examining the headings of a bookshelf. I looked at them too, over his shoulder: *hauntings, hubris, hypnosis, impotence, incompatibility.*

"I see," my father said. "You felt like it. That puts you on about the same plane as the lower primates."

"Oooh-oooh, aaaah, eee-eee." Pierce scratched under both his arms, and I swallowed my laughter.

"You kids," my father sighed. "You're making a wreck of that woman."

That woman? I thought. *You kids?* Such scornful terms for all their virtuous intent.

He directed Pierce to apologize to my mother—either in person or in writing—before he could again connect his guitar to an amplifier. Pierce solemnly gave her a note he'd folded into a tiny origami swan:

Dear Mom,

Dad says what I did to the living room makes me no better than an ape. I suppose that is the only reason I can offer you, for there is no acceptable human explanation.

Your sorry son

She kept the note beside her as she sat cross-legged on the carpet, dabbing at the stains with a bleach solution. That technique failing, she trimmed the ruined strands, one by one, as if they were wisps of a child's hair. She put them in a waxed paper bag, stashed it in one of the bureau drawers I'd searched for clues to my parents.

The Great Void

That Halloween, Pierce's costume idea—black hooded sweatshirt, black pants and shoes and gloves—had a history. When he was five and I was close to eight, we watched a *Shirley Temple Storybook* presentation called "The Terrible Clockman," an adaptation of a Jules Verne tale. The monster of the show was mostly man; his head, though, was a large metallic chunk of clock that ticked, loudly. People in the village knew they were done for when they heard the ticking coming their way. Rerun through my adult sensibilities, the Clockman seems innocuous enough, even funny, but then the bulk and sound of him scared my eyes wide open, and did the same to my brother. If one of us wanted to torment the other, we would sidle up to the bedroom doorway and click our tongue in the measured rhythm of a clock. Once, I ambushed Pierce with the ticking sounds, and he leaped, like an immense frog, from the floor to his top bunk. There was some scrabbling and grunting, but he made it up without the ladder. Another night, when Pierce repaid me with the clock torture, the hair prickled on my arms and the back of my neck, and I emitted a cry that, according to my mother, sounded like a banshee in the clothes dryer. Our parents thought the mutual fear cute and duplicated the ticking sound themselves, on occasion, to enjoy the effect it had on Pierce and me. They smiled indulgently when they comforted us.

Until Christmas. A teacher at my father's school gave us personalized alarm clocks. In addition to our names in ornamental script, she painted moon phases on the clocks, clouds, trees, apples, automobiles, ribbons, and thunderbolts. The clocks were as cute as our parents found our fear; we were told we should be grateful a virtual stranger thought enough of us to remember us with gifts. Dutifully, we wound the clocks and positioned them on our window seats.

Pierce was first to surrender, standing rigid in the hallway in front of our parents' bedroom, the clock at his feet. "Get it out of here," he screamed. "Get it out right now," over and over again, a chant for salvation.

I had lain in my bed, suffering the clock noises as they amplified in my head until I felt pain with each tick. Once Pierce blazed into the hallway, I quickly joined him, weeping loudly, holding my clock at arm's distance and running in place as though I had to pee. NO was the only word my mouth was occasionally able to form. No, stomp. No, stomp stomp. Stomp with both feet together for emphasis. No.

"What the hell," my father said, sleep rumpled. "What's the matter with you two? Didn't you have a perfect Christmas with lots of presents? Do you want us to take them away from you?"

"Yes, PLEASE," Pierce wailed. "Take these things someplace we'll never go."

"Throw them in the English Channel," I said, and believed it far enough away, deep enough. I thrust my clock in front of me like a bomb.

My father put his hands behind him and absently snapped the waist of his boxer shorts.

"The Terrible Clockman!" we said in unison.

My mother lurched out of bed, snatched the clocks, and scurried with them to the back porch as we followed. She wrapped each one in a bath towel, dropped the packets into the washing machine, closed the lid, herded us out, pulled the door shut behind her, and leaned against it. "Ta-daah," she said. "No more Clockman."

"I still hear ticking sounds," Pierce complained.

The camelback clock on the mantel. Before our own clocks, we'd noticed only the chimes.

My mother draped layers of towels over the mantel clock until we could no longer hear it from Pierce's room, where my parents let me finish out the night on the top bunk. Still, we'd been so enthralled and adrenaline-powered by fear, we had trouble going to sleep.

My father stayed in the room, attempting to calm us. "Imagine a deep hole," he said. "A dark, dark hole, and you are falling through the hole, and there is no end. Falling and falling through the great void that is endless."

We were quieted by his incantation, not his words, and he left us. I felt a weight of smooth darkness on my cheeks. I wasn't relieved; I was exhausted, pinned to the bed by the inertia of giving up after much excitement.

"Phoebe?" Pierce said, his voice unsteady. "Are you falling through the hole? Are you in the Great Void?"

"No," I whispered. "That's not very good advice. Try counting white rats instead." He hadn't yet got his pet Babushka, but he'd lobbied for her.

My mother gave the alarm clocks to Goodwill. Layer by layer, she removed towels from the camelback clock, and gradually we grew accustomed to the sound of time passing.

❄ ❄ ❄

Pierce spent half an hour in the master bathroom charcoaling his face, transforming himself into the Great Void. The double-mirror hinges squawked. My mother, drink on her nightstand, reclined on her bed. She had a new apparatus that allowed her to fall asleep sitting up without having a stiff neck later. She called it a backrest. It looked like a piece of furniture arrested at a crucial stage of development. Out of her hearing range, Pierce and I called it Thalidomide Chair. We'd used the term before, on one of her gin-bathed afternoons, and her eyes snapped open like a marionette's. "You kids are so hateful," she pronounced with the self-absorbed clarity some drunks achieve. "I can't believe I had any part in your birth." She shivered once and shut her eyes quick as she'd opened them.

I wonder now, though I didn't then, why she took her naps sitting up. What was the harm in flopping down and passing out? Perhaps she clung to a reassuring belief that an upright drunk was preferable to a prostrate one. Perhaps she thought herself readied for action if an emergency required her to spring to her feet. Or perhaps she invented a tolerable way to be involved in a family whose strongest bond was projecting the appearance of one.

Dessa and I had decided, about a week before, to dress as our mothers. Leaning against the dead tree, we cackled with insolent delight when we landed on the idea. Dessa went over to a live tree, picked a lemon, and showered bits of peel on the lawn. Then she split the fruit and we had a contest to see who could eat more lemon segments. I won. I preferred then, as I do now, tartness to sweetness.

Tina Spitz, her gym bag slung Johnny Appleseed-style on her shoulder, selected liquid amber leaves from the grass. Her father, previously from Maine (who knows what he'd done there to send him fleeing cross-continent), had arranged with the county that deciduous varieties be the only trees allowed within ten feet of the curb along our street. Tina shared her father's love of fallen leaves, and tucked them carefully into her denim sack. She also collected scraps of lemon rind.

"Um, Tina," Dessa intoned. "You realize those aren't leaves?"

"Of course," Tina said, twirling a length of her dark, oily hair. "I like color."

"Of course," Dessa said. She poked at some peelings with her feet. "My mistake."

Tina scrambled to examine these pieces and bit into one as if its flavor were a long-kept secret. Dessa and I crossed our eyes at each other.

"There," Tina said, pulling shut the drawstring of her bag. "May I come with you on Halloween?"

In a slow moving silence, Dessa and I regarded each other, then Tina, then the street. Halloween spent with the neighborhood burden? We would have rather had Pierce tag along in his enervating weirdness. Tina's request, however, stunned us—she'd barely spoken a complete sentence to us before today—and challenged our just-emerging code of social ethics. It was all right to think Tina was painfully dull, and fine to make faces and fun of her so long as she didn't notice. But it was cruel to say straight out that we didn't desire her company, that the only reason we tolerated her walking home from school with us, or straggling into our yards was because we felt sorry for her. She couldn't help that her father was a jailbird and had pretty much assured her a life on the outskirts of acceptability.

I waited for Dessa, who thought faster than I did under duress. She said, "Tina, we do things you might not approve of, you know, tricks, as in trick-or-treat, and if you were to come with us, you'd need to bring something like eggs—not the hard-boiled kind—or bar soap, or whatever." Dessa was distressingly sincere when she lied. We'd never played pranks on anyone but each other.

"Fine," Tina said. "I'll think up something."

"We don't want any of your color collection," Dessa said, broaching cruelty because she knew she was defeated.

"It's okay, I know." Tina's usual droopiness could barely accommodate the lilt in her voice. The force of it made her stagger, as if she were dizzy, when she did an about-face to go home.

Dessa clenched the remaining lemon sections till juice ran between her fingers. Her hand, like a mechanical pincer, released the pulp. "That's that," she said. "Another opportunity down the drain. No guys will talk to us with her around."

We had to be nice, we knew we had to be nice—we got this knowledge from the incongruities of our households: that unskilled photographs stayed in drawers while others, professionally posed, were displayed in hallway clusters; that mothers had coffee klatsches with neighbor women, then went home to drink liquor alone; that fathers exchanged pleasantries with other neighbor men, trimming hedges or dumping the garbage, then at the dinner table vilified them as communists or John Birchers.

I didn't tell my mother she was the inspiration for my Halloween costume. When she drank, she became alert to mockery, so I simply told her I wanted to wear something "old-fashioned, from the fifties." From her Thalidomide throne, she directed me to boxes, bags and drawers redolent of mothballs and anemic sachets. I found a goldenrod cashmere sweater, a black and gold plaid circle skirt, black pointed-toe flats.

"I saved these so you could wear them, Phoebe," she said, aglow with usefulness. "I'll put them away and save them after tonight. Long skirts and cashmere are classics. They're bound to be back in style someday."

She's not only drunk, I thought, *she's dreaming.*

Pierce then swaggered out of the bathroom, a life-size smudge of basic black. He had even covered a grocery bag with black marking pen.

"You're going as Mom," he murmured, raising his caked eyebrows. "I'm going as the Great Void. Wonder what Dad would say into his recording machine about us."

"God all Friday!" my mother said at a frequency that roused my father from his study.

He sat on the corner of a bureau and squinted above his bifocals. "Let me guess, son. A cat burglar?"

Pierce put a finger to his lips and shook his head at me. I held my hands out, empty, no clue.

"The bubonic plague? The grim reaper? No, you'd need a scythe for that. Sandra, what do you think he is?" My father spoke to her perfunctorily, as if she were a client in a group session and needed to be drawn into the fold.

"Something more subtle," she said. "A forest fire. Burnt toast. Licorice, or a blackout in New York City." She looked to my father for approval, who only regarded his son.

"Well?"

Pierce shook his head. "I'm going now."

"Without telling us?" my father said. Irritation seeped through the cracks of his convivial interrogating.

"I'm telling you," Pierce said. "I'm going."

"He's mystery," my mother sang, slugging back the dregs of her drink.

My father reached into his closet, taking from its hook his yardwork shirt, a tattered white oxford cloth. He tore a strip from it and tied it around Pierce's forearm. "You're going to wear this for visibility, whoever or whatever you are. It's dark out there."

"Now he looks like surrender," my mother said gaily, but my father gave her a sidelong glance—a slight flick of his head and eyes at the same moment—that iced her enthusiasm. "We don't want you hit by a car."

I shadowed Pierce down the hallway. "Can I tell them, yes or no?"

"Go ahead," he said, already undoing the armband. "But wait till I'm completely gone." He dropped the rag into his sack, which, I saw, had a towel rolled on the bottom.

"What's in the towel?" I asked, nudging his arm. "Eggs? Soap? Razor blades?"

"Yeah," he said. "Stuff." He walked past the picture windows and Volare, not recognizing him, bayed like a bloodhound. "Must be an excellent disguise," he said, and walked off into the patchy black of the streets.

As I watched him merge with a silhouetted group, I was ambushed by a brief sorrow. Here was my brother, my strange little brother, embarking on what promised to be a strange adolescence, and he was embarking without me. I already knew most of adolescence happened away from home, even though we slept and dressed and ate there.

"Do you want to know who he was, still?" I said to my parents, who pretended to ignore each other, my father ripping the rest of his shirt into cleaning cloths, my mother tamping her cigarette on the arm of her stunted chair.

They raised their eyes to me.

"The Great Void." I grinned at the memories it conjured and at being able to say it without terror.

My parents looked lost, mouths barely agape, as if understanding might be taken in like food.

"Is that a rock band?" my father said, and my mother chuckled. She knew what the Great Void wasn't, but not what it was.

❀ ❀ ❀ ❀

A stylish brunette approached Dessa and me as we waited in the grainy wash of a streetlight. The girl wore a Rudy Gernreich-inspired multi-paneled shift, white go-go boots, and bangle bracelets. Her hair was cinched up into a cluster of loops accented by grosgrain ribbon, spit curls plastered on the skin by either ear. Her eyeliner was expertly done, a black swath over the eyelashes with an identical swath of glimmery white above the black. She wore pink lipstick flecked with sparkles. When she reached into her gym bag, I knew who she was.

"My dad gave me two cans of shaving cream," Tina said. "He went electric."

Dessa held the tiara in her hair as if it were a handle for maintaining equilibrium. "My lord," she said. "Tina, you look stupendous."

"Thanks, yeah, my mother dressed me. I usually won't let her. Dad says I could be her double. You guys look pretty, um, different."

Dessa wore a billowy black crepe formal with a crushed red velvet bolero. My mother had insisted I wear vermilion lipstick to complete my fifties look. The three of us resembled a pageant of fashion through the years, Dessa and I representing *Then* and Tina *Now*.

Tina's mother did her shopping in Encino, groceries included; no one had seen much more of her than the view from her shoulders up as she careened down the street in her silver Cadillac. I realized, from Tina's costume, that Mrs. Spitz was an aging teenybopper. I'd had teachers like her—women in their thirties and forties who loped around campus in short skirts and poorboy sweaters, clinging to their youth with spikey lacquered fingernails—and they made me nervous. I felt that, underneath their trendy fashion choices, they envied me the years I had to avoid the mistakes they had made. My favorite teacher was in her twenties and wore sedate wool and linen suits. She pronounced "the Commutative Property of numbers" with such authority that I listened closer to her lectures, in case she'd say those words again.

Dessa and I had pitied Tina Spitz her ex-convict father; tonight I pitied her more for her mother.

I brought along a stash of sycamore pods to use as grenades if we needed them.

Our first half hour out, a group of Vespucci marauders hooted at Dessa and me, whistled derisively at Tina, whom they called "Puss in Boots," lobbed some eggs in our path, then ditched us. No longer gawkily amusing when we dressed up, and not yet sophisticated either, we must have been a stinging sight to anyone but our parents, who were as used to us as they were to each other. I wanted to bomb these loud-mouth boys who wore jeans and T-shirts—no costumes for us to ridicule—but I could envision how pathetic we'd look, wearing finery on our budding women's bodies and behaving like children. We'd be no better than my teachers who flirted with staying young.

We needed a consummate victim, being vulnerable ourselves. Dessa indicated Mrs. Winifred Hellmun's driveway, and our heads dipped and bobbed in agreement. Three of us could handle one of her.

Winnie Hellmun was a ten-year widow in a community from which most widows felt compelled to move. Her only child, a daughter, got pregnant and married young, and Mrs. Hellmun's bad luck and solitude made neighbors suspicious. Her nickname was Winnie the Shrew, and there were rumors. She carefully tended the lollipop-shaped rose trees that lined both sides of her driveway, and had allegedly chased a neighbor off her property for stopping to admire and sniff a particular sunrise-tinged bloom. One version of the story had Winnie wielding a hoe. Also, she reportedly polished the individual leaves of her ivy ground cover, vacuumed her driveway, and dusted the interior of her mailbox, which was a miniature replica of her house.

Winnie Hellmun, over years of being scrutinized by a neighborhood hungry for anything other than quiet uniformity, became what we expected her to become: a manageable eccentric. I once saw her deliver a benediction for a gopher she'd trapped. "The Lord giveth and the Lord taketh away," she said, shaking the furry remains into a garbage can, and I believed this proof of her insanity rather than a symptom of her loneliness.

Dessa, Tina, and I pressed the bell several times to ensure she'd be harried when she reached the door. "Triiick orrrr treeeat," we said, drawing out each word.

Winnie poked her steely head into the wedge of space the open door formed. "Too old," she said. "Too old for Halloween, too young to be dressed like hookers." She shut the door and turned off her porch light.

Dessa chewed on her hair, contemplating revenge; I chucked a sycamore puff bomb onto the immaculate drive; Tina's chest heaved, I thought, at the prospect of inflicting trouble rather than enduring it.

"Here," she said, thrusting a shaving cream can at Dessa. "Ready, go." She ran to the ivy bank, high-stepping it in her boots, spraying white spirals over the heart-shaped leaves. "Never too old!" she said, like a battle cry.

Radiantly rid of her self, Tina frightened Dessa and me out of our zeal for retribution. We stopped after spelling *shrew* in menthol cream on the drive, studding it with the petals of a rose big as the head of a baby. We waited for Tina, who didn't look as if her frenzy would soon abate.

"What now?" Dessa said. "Do we leave her? Let her roll till her ammo runs out?"

"No," I said, for at that moment Winnie reopened her door and opened fire on us with hard candies. Her aim was true and her arm pelting strong. We flanked Tina, each wresting an arm, and escorted her off the property. She craned her neck to have a final glance at her handiwork.

As peacocks shrieked her arrival, we deposited Tina at the gate of her house, where she asked, "Why can we only do this once a year?"

❀ ❀ ❀ ❀

My mother sat with her hands folded primly on the kitchen table. She typically had pink blotches, from the gin, across her nose and cheeks. Tonight she was grey-faced, and my father's Volkswagen was gone from the driveway.

"It's Pierce," she said. I remembered how curiously sad I'd been as he wandered into the neighborhood's darkness. "Barely twelve and in handcuffs."

I wasn't an accomplished sleeper, yet that night I fell into a willful slumber. Pierce was safe and alive, of that I was certain—they didn't, after all, handcuff corpses. I slept so I wouldn't have to see my father, the vapid glare of confusion in his normally assured eyes, when they arrived home. He'd have a plan by morning, I knew, and I did not care to see him that night.

As I slept, I dreamed Pierce in handcuffs and leg irons. He wept without shame and yelled at the police, "You can't build enough fences. You can't shut out the wilderness," and he still spoke with a lisp.

Deviled Eggs

The sky went slate-grey with feeble light behind it, and I let myself into Pierce's room. He was awake, transistor earphone in place, the volume up so loud I could hear the lyrics of the Yardbirds' song he was mouthing about shapes of things before his eyes. He lay propped on pillows in the bottom bunk. A pencil in hand, every so often he reached up and wrote, "fuck fuck fuck fuck fuck fuck," across a support slat beneath the upper mattress.

"Do you want to talk about it?" I said, and he answered me with tears, vivid Pierce tears, spurting from the corners of his eyes. I held his left hand for a long time. The hand had lost its pudginess, but still smelled of a child's skin: reheated dirt and sweat. He continued to deface the slat, and I watched the sky turn a blue as unreal as the color of paint for sick trees.

❋ ❋ ❋ ❋

"This is the first of what I hope will be many family meetings." My father actually had note cards, and referred to them from time to time, flipping the used ones under the rim of his dinner plate. "We've lost touch with each other, and we need to reconvene."

I had once heard Dessa use the expression, "No shit, Sherlock," and it now danced on the tip of my tongue, which I kept still.

"We all know what happened," my father read on, "and this is what is going to be."

My mother stared into her drink, and Pierce into the thick oleander bush outside the mullioned window. I almost wished I had forced myself to witness my father's confusion the night before so that I could forgive him his present brash authority.

For unknown reasons, my father suffered occasional sciatica. ("The human back is capricious as the human brain," his orthopedist explained.) The condition bent and hobbled him like a young character actor playing an older man. He snubbed medication during the day and took Darvon at night so he could sleep. "The quality of sleep determines the quality of life," he was fond of saying. He kept the pills in the master bathroom medicine cabinet.

While in that bathroom, Pierce, putting the finishing touches on his Great Void disguise, also absconded with a full bottle of my father's Darvon.

I ran a mental film of the story as Pierce told it to me the morning I held his hand. He hitchhikes down Wells Drive to the Tarzana/Encino border, where koi ponds are veritable moats around homes and property costs just as exclusive. There, he joins other members of the garage band he's begun to play in. A group of squeaky kids hike up a hilly, just-paved side street of scraped naked lots, cramped adobe wedges worth tens of thousands. A bath towel spreads before them onto which they throw cigarettes, a clear pint of peppermint schnapps, a green bottle of vermouth, a baggie of grass from someone's older sister recently dropped out of college, ZigZag papers thin as insect wings and equally as hard to handle without tearing, and an auburn prescription bottle of Darvon capsules. Unbelievable, the bounty of teamwork and home investigation.

A beat-up VW van chugs to a halt alongside them. Maybe the van is a little too ramshackle, as if someone purposely took a baseball bat to it. Three guys empty out. They have long hair, maybe too long for their clean-shaven faces. Psychedelic clothing, maybe too loud a geometric print on one's pants, too many weird appliqués on one's jean jacket, too many strands of glass beads around the neck of the other. Maybe they say, "Far out," a little too much or too enthusiastically. So that, when the one in the jacket asks how much per pill, Pierce bolts.

Down the new sidewalk, the vacant lots go by like giant stairsteps in his peripheral vision. Down, down until he hears the whir of the coasting van and hurls himself into the deep iceplant of the first landscaped house he comes to. He flattens like an animal rug. With a flashlight, they spot a symmetrical blot of black, and apply the cuffs.

"Please, PLEASE," Pierce says. "Don't call my parents," but my father's name and address are neatly affixed to the painkiller bottle.

❀ ❀ ❀ ❀

"So, big man," my father said, passing the tamale pie. "Big outlaw. Here's what you can look forward to, unless, of course, you'd rather deal with the juvenile authorities," and he delineated the next six years of my brother's life.

Classical acoustic guitar lessons, but no more electric, no more garage bands, no bands, period, unless affiliated with the school. The boys he'd kept company with of late obviously weren't worth the time their parents took to soak their dirty diapers. If Pierce didn't like this arrangement, he could simply do without the guitar. Forever, as far as our father was concerned.

Pierce would maintain an A average in his solid subjects throughout junior and senior high. If he fell below that standard, he'd be grounded until his grades improved.

"There's no reason for you to achieve less than superior grades," my father said, tapping a note card emphatically with his index finger. "I've checked the records. Both you kids have intelligence quotients to be thankful for and honored."

My mind saw a younger Pierce, kneeling beside his bunk beds, hands pressed together and eyes squeezed shut, saying,

"God bless Mom and Dad and Volare and Phoebe and, especially, my IQ." My mother saw me smirking and flicked my kneecap under the table.

Pierce would become involved in school activities: a service club, or he could run for student government. In high school, the same general plan, plus he'd go out for a sport. "You might consider track and field, since you're so enamored of running."

Pierce winced and pronged an olive on his plate.

All of this was, of course, intended for Pierce's own benefit. He'd have a home with us rather than with the reprobates at juvie hall. He'd be accepted to a UC campus; he'd have a fruitful life. He would not be just another casualty of dope. If he kept his act clean, his police file would be sealed when he was eighteen.

And there was something else, something that might feel like punishment but was a matter of practicality and humanity. Volare. Pierce had already demonstrated he had priorities other than caring for the dog—walking him, combing him, shoveling and bagging his crap. Certainly, with the new order of goals and behavior, Pierce would have even less time to devote to Volare. Our mother had enough to do in the realm of housework, and the aging dog would require more exercise and attention than Pierce could expect to have the time to give. Volare would have to go.

Pierce blanched and trembled so, he had to set his fork down. "You're putting a dog to sleep because I got arrested?"

"No, son. We're not killing him. We're giving him to a family who can care for him as much as he deserves."

I also trembled. Pierce and I manifested this symptom we then associated with nervousness but which had more to do with a rage we could not direct. Our parents had meticulously fashioned our existence like an ornamental egg, bedecking it in paint and polish, degrees and expectations, emptying it of untidy substance. Neither Pierce nor I was cruel enough to reach out and smash the hollow thing. With a diligence that rivaled our parents' decorative fervor, we gouged and picked at its surface, yet we couldn't ruin the fragile, florid beauty we identified as love.

"Wait a second, Dad," I said, my voice wobbly as a warped record. "The dog belongs to all of us. I'll take responsibility for him, for a while, at least."

"I've made the arrangements," my father said. "We'll drop him off this Sunday at a ranch in Thousand Oaks. Besides, Phoebe, you start senior high next fall. You'll have interests that conflict with dog care."

"Martin," my mother said, her eyes inert with disbelief. "This isn't what I meant. I meant for Volare to stay and have more kindness. I didn't mean we should ship him out like an old uncle."

"The ranch idea, Sandra, is best for everyone, including the dog. And now Pierce knows how his mistakes affect the entire family." My father straightened the stack of cards. "You'll remember this, won't you, son?"

"Yes, I will," Pierce said, drawing his elbows and hands to his torso, as if to contain his inner shaking. "Always."

❦ ❦ ❦

It wouldn't have done to simply open the station wagon's tailgate, coax Volare out, and drive off into his past. There had to be a picnic, a splendid one with thick sliced ham sandwiches on extra sour delicatessen rye, my mother's homemade bleu cheese potato salad, turtle brownies variegated with caramel, a thermos jug of minted iced tea. Pierce and I scampered with Volare up and down the sandstone formations of Chatsworth Park. We played keep away with a tennis ball. We fed him at least a dozen deviled egg halves and my mother did the same, stroking his silky ears. Every now and then my father held Volare's muzzle in both hands and scratched him gruffly under the chin. In off moments when no one fed or romped with or cuddled the dog, his ears pressed to his head and he regarded us inquisitively: what was the source of this orgy of food and affection?

The drive to Thousand Oaks was a quiet one. Tears slicked Pierce's face and mine, but neither of us sobbed. We knew how to mourn without histrionics. My father pulled the station wagon alongside a smallish, prefabricated green and white barn. He shook hands with a man in a beige Stetson and a belt buckle large as a fist. My mother stayed in the car and opened the separate thermos she'd managed to avoid until that difficult moment. Pierce and I walked Volare to the edge of an alfalfa pasture.

My brother crouched beside the dog, his arms clear around his belly. "Bite horses and cows on the ankles," he said. "Suck eggs in the hen house. Cause some problems, and have a good life."

Volare's ears pricked up. He held his nose high to the aromas, strange vegetation, and animal dung. He cocked his tail like a skunk on parade and trotted out into the plants that were taller than he was.

My mind froze a shot of the proud mongrel whose image comes back to me now and again, a grown person often too smug or self-contained to know she needs memory as much as a child needs a name, or a traveler a destination and map.

THE IMPERVIOUSNESS OF ELBOW SKIN

IN THE INTERIM YEARS BEFORE Pierce reached high school, my main contact with him was in the backyard pool shack where we explored our thresholds of physical pain. The imperviousness of elbow skin got him started.

"Amazing!" he said, waving me into the bamboo-wrapped cabana. He clipped a clothespin to the flaccid skin at either of his elbows. "It doesn't even hurt; it's practically numb."

I rolled up my sweater sleeves and he similarly pinned my elbow skin. Then he attached clothespins to his earlobes and put some on mine. Dessa came over and adorned herself with pins in the same places we'd put them, suggesting we also try the web of skin between our thumbs and index fingers. She studied her wristwatch; we wore the clothespins for an hour and thirty-three minutes as we discussed the phenomenon of mind over body, men who walked on hot coals without suffering burns, who stuck blades through their cheeks without bleeding, who relaxed on beds of sharp volcanic rock.

Our endurance trials added a new challenge each time we met. We donned our clothespins, and pulled a hair from our heads every ten minutes. Plucking the hair wasn't as painful as the anticipation of having to pluck with regularity. To intermittent hair pulling, we tacked on the raucous static from Pierce's untuned transistor radio. Then a particular cheap brand of incense that was supposed to approximate jasmine but came closer to smoldering barf, and then the continuous sucking of ice cubes until our eyes watered and clenched from the jabs of pain behind them. Then we threaded monofilament line through a needle and strung together the calloused tips of our fingers, then we conjured atrocities we hoped we'd never perceive: the thud of a loved one hit by a car, the stench of bodies fried by radioactivity, the hard barrel of a gun pressed against the tender skin of our palates. Or even opening our eyes and seeing nothing, not even the speckled lights that played beneath our lids when we couldn't sleep, not even darkness. Nothing. Clear, unbroken nothing.

Like the Twelve Days of Christmas of minimalized torture, our regimen had the appeal of invention and reenactment. No doubt experts would call what we did a mild form of self-abuse, but we were served by it. We meted out the pain, defined its cause and symptom, and occasionally laughed at how absurd we looked—clothespinned, sewn, massaging our cold-cramped brows—as we invoked our own moderate suffering.

Dessa and I quit the cabana routine when we found jags of missing hair along the stems of our scrupulously trained center parts. Flirting with pain was one thing; flirting with baldness another. Pierce quit too, because, in his words, "No such thing as forbearing torture alone. Someone has to be there to notice."

❀ ❀ ❀

A short time later at the dinner table, my father paid our mother the culinary tribute she'd long awaited and ceased expecting.

"You actually make zucchini palatable, Sandra. Nothing short of wizardry." He savored a mouthful, looking thoughtfully at a corner of the ceiling, then asked, "What's the crunchy stuff on top?"

"French fried onion rings," she said softly. "Canned." The shock on her face waned to bewildered gratitude; her fingers encircled his wrist and she rested her forearm on his.

Forks poised over our dinner plates, Pierce and I sat transfixed. Our parents touching at the evening meal? This was tantamount to their arguing in ranges louder than profound hissing or taking nude photographs of each other. My father gazed studiously at his caressed arm, as though he were watching the industry and struggle of an anthill, then he removed my mother's arm and placed it next to his on the table. He patted the arm to make known he wanted it to stay where he had laid it. All shock and gratitude vanished from my mother's face, which returned to its usual alcoholic glaze.

Pierce and I dared not look at each other. We asked to be excused and pushed our chairs in behind us. We calmly walked down the hall to my room, the farthest from the kitchen. We closed the door, crawled into my closet, and slid the doors partway shut. Seated among my sneakers and heels and suede flats, we laughed the hysterical laughter of sadness, of having seen a wretched, real moment as if through a window or keyhole, as if we had intentionally spied.

"I didn't know they needed that sort of contact," I sputtered, nervously hugging a shoe.

"They probably don't know it either," Pierce said, wiping his eyes. "That's why husbands and wives have kids like us. To be their witnesses."

THE CORE

PIERCE KEPT HIS GRADES UP. He excelled at acoustic guitar and my father relented a little, allowing Pierce to take electric lessons, jazz only, none of that Jimi Hendrix desecration of the national anthem. He found a niche on the journalism staff and went out for track. Throughout high school, he smoked cigarettes and dope, nestled in his tree house, a pallet inside the lushest orange tree on our property. Dessa and I frequently joined him in what we called "The Core," a smooth pocket Pierce had carved within the tree's foliage. Sitting in this center of green under the introspective influence of cannabis, we imagined ourselves the seeds of a large exotic fruit, the nucleus of a cell ready to divide, the speedy electrons of an atom. Inside The Core, we found ourselves by losing ourselves.

One contemplative afternoon, Pierce burst forth with, "If I can understand the energy of all matter, I should be able to win a fucking foot race."

We giggled at the non-sequitur, its unasked for truth and possibility, and our eyes shone like doll eyes fresh from the factory.

Lacking a compelling reason such as terror or escape, Pierce was only an average runner. He didn't have the endurance for the longer events, and when he passed or accepted the baton in a relay, it was often more of a two-man juggling routine than a display of swiftness and coordination. His best event was the hundred-yard dash. He didn't have to run far, yet he had time enough to pick up speed, and didn't have to worry about anything but velocity—no curves, no hand-offs.

Fueled by his tree fort proclamation, Pierce nearly won a race the day my father rescheduled his afternoon appointments so that he could observe his son.

I sat beside my father in the bleachers of Grove High's ivy-festooned stadium. The parents there—as many as it took to fill about a ten-by-twenty-foot section of seating—seemed as tense and vicariously interested as my father, who clenched his jaw, rippling the skin of his cheeks, and tapped the tips of his long fingers to a rhythm he had in his head. Other parents chewed gum and sunflower seeds, folded and shredded wrappers and fliers, repeatedly made sure their hairstyles were in place, pulled at their socks, checked their wristwatches, coughed, and cleared their throats. All of them hoped their sons would win and were nervous about that hope, since most would depart suffering loss.

Pierce, in the starting blocks, was a looping of arms and legs, having begun the growth spurt that would stretch him to six foot three. Before the gun, he glanced in our direction and tossed back his mane of brown hair. The gesture was defiant and endearing; the longhaired look rankled my father, yet no other boy in the blocks gave the slightest indication he knew he had an audience. At the shot, Pierce broke ahead.

He remained ahead almost the entire race. My father's fingertips pressed vehemently together, bowing the fingers and purpling the nails. Other parents hollered admonitions and encouragements to their sons, but my father remained silent. This was the closest I ever saw him to the attitude of prayer.

Fifteen feet before the finish line, Pierce's left leg buckled and he fell forward, first onto his knees, then hands, then chin and face. My father's palms separated and gripped his thighs. There was a collective sound of pity, a muffled "Awww," from the stands around us. The toe of Pierce's right shoe pounded his frustration into the gravelly dirt behind him, and he stayed in the dirt until the other contestants cleared the track. A timekeeper, the magenta-nosed French teacher who supposedly kept a flask of vodka in a coat hanging in her classroom, helped Pierce up and off the course. He limped slightly, and had abrasions on his knees, but he was intact.

"Goddamn him," my father said under his breath. "Goddamn that boy. He fell on purpose."

Whether my father was right is immaterial—he believed what he believed. Pierce maintained that a sharp cramp in his left calf had dropped him to his knees. My father scoffed at his son's explanation; Pierce wouldn't confess to losing intentionally, and consequently neither could approach the other with trust. They resorted to an avoidance, mutual and consuming, and paid more attention to each other than they ever had before.

"They watch each other like beasts in the wild," my mother drawled, wringing her dishcloth. From the kitchen window, she studied Pierce and my father, their wordless, mechanical pruning of our citrus trees and cautious bundling of the thorny branches.

Liquor no longer soothed my mother—it competed with her family and household for the privilege of wearing her down. She lurked on the back porch, ostensibly folding laundry, or ironing, or reading a new recipe book she'd ordered from *Time/Life*. For the most part, though, she leaned against the tile counter, drinking gin from a tempered-glass measuring cup. She didn't fuss with tonic water or ice cubes anymore. Her skin and hair were the same dull shade, somewhere between gold and grey. I missed the days when she had cocktail mixing routines, bursts of vibrant energy, then went to sleep sitting up.

❀ ❀ ❀ ❀

At the end of our junior year, Dessa and I bemoaned our sporadic dates, the paltry kissing skills of the boys we went out with, the ugliness of hickeys, the shame of our virginity, and our general lack of popularity. We analyzed each other's body and skin types, the shapes of our faces, the propriety of our hairdos. We concluded that, while neither of us was beautiful, we weren't unattractive. Dessa was what my mother had once called "striking"—tall, leggy, her chestnut hair accentuating her coltishness; I was shorter, nearer the ground—"well-rounded," my mother euphemized—and my olive coloring mistaken by some as a year-round tan. Why did all the wrong boys notice us, the ones who kissed with the finesse of moray eels, the ones who asked, "Do you want to do it?" instead of leading us to the brink where there was no question?

Stoned in the tree fort, Dessa and I discussed normalcy. We thought perhaps if we indulged in a normal teenage phase we'd be construed as normal ourselves, rather than the pariahs we seemed to be. If we formed a Van Morrison fan club, or volunteered for candy stripers, or had nervous breakdowns from excessive studying, or ran for cheerleading, maybe we would feel part of the high school experience that till then had eluded us. We were too analytical to accept as normal the insidious desire to be other than who we were, and too jaded to believe we could effect any genuine change. Instead, we dabbled in makeup: tiny brushes to outline our lips, fake lashes for top lids, trimmed segments for the bottom, translucent powder for our oily noses and orangey blush for our emerging cheekbones.

Pierce squinted at us one day in The Core and said, "You guys look about thirty-five or thirty-eight."

"Good," Dessa said, rolling her eyes behind the weighty lashes. "Maybe guys will stop asking for permission."

Pierce passed me the joint and said, "Yeah, but you better promise each other you won't let this makeup bullshit soak through your faces and pickle your brains."

I shook Dessa's hand. "I solemnly swear to remain forever your friend, Phoebe Dunn."

Dessa swore the same allegiance to herself and me, her voice catching slightly on the dope smoke.

❀ ❀ ❀ ❀

Four months later at my front door, Dessa delineated for me the loss of her virginity: "My head was between the armrest and the window lever. The gearshift mashed my thigh and the brake dug into the base of my spine. I barely noticed when my hymen broke."

"God," I cringed, not sure whether the subject matter or the chemicals in the lash glue made my eyes water. "I'll devote my life to studying the mating rites of birds, preferably those doomed to extinction. Terrence can be my illustrator."

"Phoebe, the quality improves with practice. All the books say so. It's something you have to get over with, like standing in line at the DMV to get your learner's permit."

"Nice analogy, Dess. Think Terrence and I'll just continue rolling around with clothes on."

I met Terrence Lambert, the non-athletic son of Grove High's football coach, in health class. Terrence had the most extravagant real eyelashes I'd ever seen on anyone, male or female—they were dark, backward-curling waves. He was a gifted sketcher, and wooed me by drawing cartoons of my likeness in a cheerleading uniform, the G crooked on my sweater, the hem falling out of my skirt, my shoelaces untied. My caricature pondered matters far removed from school spirit: the proliferation of troops in Vietnam, the avarice of the middle and upper classes, the hysterical propaganda in the anti-drug films our health teacher screened at least once a week. Terrence's cartoons helped ease my dissatisfaction with who I was; in fact, I probably loved his consoling perceptions of me more than I loved Terrence himself. His affection for me might also have sprung from the need to be consoled. In a letter he wrote after we broke up, he said, "I loved you because you were the first decent-looking girl to treat me as something other than a study aid." I'm astonished how warped desires often fit well beside each other, like oddly shaped shoes in a narrow box.

In his mother's Cougar, Terrence and I parked on the new-ly bulldozed streets of Chalk Hill, kissed until our lips chafed the color of plums, petted until our hands cramped when we arrived at simultaneous climax, each in our own bucket seat. Occasionally, when my father was out of town giving or taking a seminar, we'd ascertain my mother's snoring, then borrow the study. On the floor, our upper bodies bare and lower clothed, we writhed and wriggled over each other like hatching insects, pink blotching our faces and damp spreading across the front of Terrence's jeans. He brought a sweatshirt to tie around his waist, in case he ran into anyone as he left my house or returned to his own.

In the relative safety and comfort of the study, I'd begged Terrence to unzip himself and me and go the distance, and he invariably refused.

"I'm scared I'll hurt you, Phoebe," he said. "I don't want to make you ashamed or pregnant, and besides, we're doing this for the pleasure. Which we're obviously getting."

I'm still touched by his considerateness, in the same way I'm touched by old movies whose happy endings exceed the limits of my idealism. Dessa, however, thought his self-control indicated psychological problems, and urged me to find someone with a normal sex drive.

"You know what the song says, Phoebe—'Ain't nothing like the real thing, baby.'"

I stared hard at my friend, who sat on the brick steps of my house, where I'd seen her hundreds of afternoons before. She twirled a rope of her hair and half smirked at me, crossing her legs demurely at the ankles. I realized she was readying herself for the world of appearances, of adulthood. I trembled at how easily she succumbed, how languorously she tabled her mind and celebrated her body, the mere container for all that made Dessa Dessa. I, who would abide adulthood faltering and squirming, envied her the grace that risked complacency.

"You're so full of yourself, I'm shocked you can accommodate sex," I said, and turned and went inside.

In a little while, Pierce came into my room, bug-eyed and earnest, and sat next to me on my bed. "What did you say to Dessa? She came up to The Core and practically inhaled a whole joint by herself. Now she's blubbering like Mom before she got used to booze, or it got used to her, or whatever." He poked my side.

"Dessa's a loss to makeup and guys," I said past a quaver in my voice. "She could smoke a kilo and it wouldn't matter."

"Even so, Phoebe, she's your only best friend." Pierce, quirky as he was, remained orthodox about loyalties. For years, he sent a Christmas card to Volare's ranch, and commemorated the day of Babushka's death by blacking out that square on his desk calendar.

I trusted Pierce's instincts as I trusted my own mind. Our mother and father clothed and fed and sheltered us, but Pierce and I were spiritual godparents to each other. Both of us breathed the unique unhappiness that pervaded the air of our house, rampant as the dust my mother battled, covert as my father's musings into a tape machine. Pierce and I encoded secrets no one else on earth would understand or have need to. There was no trick in belonging to a family; the difficulty lay in the maze we followed out of the snare of belonging. Dessa, I reminded myself, had no brother or sister and wended her way out alone.

I relented. I stood in the tree well below The Core and apologized to Dessa, said I'd been cruel because her innuendo put in question Terrence's masculinity.

I lied, of course. My reaction had nothing to do with innuendo or masculinity or Terrence. I was losing my friend, and blamed her entirely for a progression neither of us could stop much less verbalize. Many friendships, I've since found, start to end with the promise that they won't.

❋ ❋ ❋ ❋

There is virtually no fall in Southern California but a dry, drawn out summer. Leaves drop, helped along by scathing Santa Ana winds, and in late November or early December, the air turns mildly cold. I have a theory that strange things happen in October because the absence of season impels people toward changes of their own.

When I remember the October we were seniors, I do so with a sense that Dessa and I bided our time, less said between us than ever before, perhaps in anticipation of the gaping silence that remains when a friendship is over. We spent hours simply lounging: on the front steps, in The Core, or on the lawn at the base of the dead grapefruit tree. We read and reread teen magazines, checked our faces in compact mirrors, listened to 93 KHJ boss radio on a transistor, daydreamed about our next or latest tryst. We each secretly blamed the other for our boredom.

One afternoon, we watched Tina Spitz, who continued to study leaf color, but no longer collected the leaves. She'd discarded her gym bag altogether; now she held the leaves close to her face as if she memorized their mottled color schemes. Then with great care, she put each leaf back where she'd found it, in precisely the same position. She took as much time to replace a leaf as she did to examine it. Dessa and I exchanged glances that meant we associated Tina's tenderness with her abnormality.

Dessa picked a piece of brittle bark from the dead tree. "Oh, look," she said, in mock wonder. "This bark is shaped exactly like a cloud."

"And this," I said, peeling off another piece, "is a smoke signal."

"Here is an amoeba," Dessa said.

I returned, "Here is a lump of clay."

If Tina caught the drift of our satirical game, she forgot it the moment we were assailed by a sound—my mother bellowing the word *No*—from the closed garage. We moved haltingly in the direction of the door, and again heard the distressing noise that was both my mother and a terror, huge and feral, larger than she or the garage could hold. I opened the garage door, whose springs complained in a hollow rumble, to let the clamoring out.

I first saw my mother, gone silent, standing on the concrete step that led from her back porch down into the garage. At ninety-degree angles to her hips, her hands splayed out like talons. Her mouth alternately outlined the empty shape of an oval and a rectangle, and refused to close.

Next, I saw the dirty bottoms of Pierce's white crew socks, drifting midair, occasionally kicking above an orange crate toppled on the concrete floor. I followed the sock bottoms to his brown corduroy jeans, to the dark moles on his tawny back, to his neck. Through his hair, the neck flared an angry reddish purple, caught in the leather hand-hold of a dog leash. His face, too, was red, twitching with pain, his hands marked by the chain they clutched above his head.

"Please," he hissed. "PLEASE. I'm afraid to let go."

Dessa did not move. I did not move. My mother's hands balled to fists, then splayed out again, but the rest of her, aside from the slight change in shape her mouth made, didn't budge. We knew the wrong move would kill him.

Tina Spitz stepped out of the background up to the orange crate, which she righted, and to which she guided and flattened Pierce's feet.

"Keep them there," she said, and slapped them as a mother would slap a naughty child's hand. She pulled a sawhorse over so she could step up and gently slip his head from the chain and leather noose. With the gravity she reserved for leaf gathering, she descended the sawhorse and eased Pierce to the floor.

"Don't ever do that again," she said brusquely.

Pierce, eyes vaguely contrite even in their pain, took three steps on the concrete and his legs folded like paper beneath him.

Then my mother rushed to him, then Tina moved aside and leaned against the hat stand joined to the bicycle. Dessa covered her mouth and lurched into the side yard where we kept our garbage cans. I ran for the phone.

❋ ❋ ❋

Pierce spent a week in St. Joseph's psychiatric ward, his neck sprained, not broken. The permanent damage occurred to his larynx where his vocal chords had crushed and ruptured; when they healed, their scarring reduced his voice to a hoarse whisper. As a result, Pierce had two therapists: one for his spirit, one for his elocution.

The speech therapist, who specialized in self-inflicted injury (one of her patients, my parents told me, had removed half his face with a shotgun), attempted to train Pierce to swallow air and form words with the resulting emissions. He objected.

"Sounds more like yorking than talking." The therapist next tried machinery, a battery-operated box with a microphone that amplified Pierce's syllables into twangs resembling Jew's harp music. He became accomplished at scat singing with the contraption, but never trusted it as a substitute for his voice.

One night, he unstrapped the box from his shoulder, wrapped the microphone cord around the main unit, and put it all in the wastebasket under the kitchen sink. He turned to us, where we watched dumbfoundedly from the table, and said, "I did this to myself. This is me, this is how I talk. Get used to it."

Throughout Pierce's week at the hospital, his counseling appointments and recovery, my parents rarely confided in me, except regarding the speech therapist's morbid credentials. Mostly, when they felt my eyes asking them for comfort, they would tell me how glad they were he was alive. They inclined nearer each other, as if their forced proximity would reassure me.

Pierce eventually yanked misfortune by the seat of its pants and made it advantage; he wrote an editorial titled, "The Travesty of High School Sports: For Every Win, Ten Injuries," that would garner him an *LA Times* journalism scholarship to Berkeley. Thus, he fulfilled my father's plan, though not precisely as my father wanted, not in a way of which he was wholly proud. My father said, "This article is a glorified excuse for failure," when the piece debuted in the *Grove High Gazette.*

And when my brother married, he kept the ceremony in Northern California, safe from our family. Pierce sent pictures of the wizened, grinning Pomo couple that stood up for him and Nola, his exquisitely tall and kind-eyed wife with whom he transcribes dying Native American languages. In one photograph, the four pose like ascending stairs beside a bend in the Russian River. "His own parents and home weren't good enough," my father commented. "He had to have Indians and a river."

❀ ❀ ❀ ❀

A long friendship doesn't dissolve in a moment, but certain moments contribute to its dissolution. One blustery November afternoon, about a month after what we called The Dog Leash Problem, Dessa and I went for a walk. We didn't linger in The Core; it seemed like trespassing or sacrilege now to claim as ours a place Pierce had hollowed out for himself. Usually, we sat on the lawn beneath the dead tree, but that day the air was so turbulent I suppose Dessa and I felt the urge to move.

She yammered on about her boyfriend, a shot-putter whose shoulder width dwarfed his height. They'd switched from doing it in his dad's car to making love in her canopy bed. She would create a lot of bathroom noise—faucets running, toilet flushing—while he climbed through her un-latched bedroom window.

"I'm spooked, though," Dessa said, holding her hair from the wind as if it were a hat with a veil. "My window screen is getting all bent out of shape and Daddy Otto noticed it last weekend. He almost called the police because he thought someone tried to rob us." She cackled in a rich, mischievous tone, and waited for my response.

Which was slow. Since The Dog Leash Problem, I was preoccupied, worried that Pierce, bright as he was, would find a surer way of killing himself: a gun, a cliff, or poison. I was afraid to talk to him about it, afraid to remind him of an episode I irrationally hoped he'd forget, and deathly afraid of what the off-white house would be without him. Dessa knew me well enough to bristle at the cause of my distraction.

"God, Phoebe. Is the wind blowing my voice away, or what?" She shook my shoulder, and I pulled aside.

"What do you want me to do—volunteer to fix the screen?" I cocked my eyebrow at her and kept on walking.

"Drop it," she said. "Get over this mood you're in or people at school will think you're as lost as your brother. Even my mom says suicide is a coward's way out."

I stood still in my tracks. "And what do you think, Dessa?"

As if the matter of suicide weren't worthy of much more discussion, she shrugged and said, "I pretty much agree."

"Right," I said. "That's why you puked at the scene."

I did an about face, and we walked home in a kinetically

charged silence. Dessa lagged a few paces behind me, perhaps resenting my infernal pensiveness, or being tied to a friend with a family as unsuccessful at tragedy as mine. Had Pierce actually killed himself, Dessa and her mother and a procession of other neighborhood women would have buried us in Bundt cakes and casseroles.

But I wasn't concerned with her judgment of me and what I came from. As I broke through the gusts we faced into, I recalled Dessa stealing her mother's tiara from its pillow atop the piano, Dessa at the uppermost crook of the dead tree, Dessa as her mother on Halloween, and I suddenly saw our child's play as rehearsal for the primary decisions of adulthood: Do we become our parents or don't we? Can we possibly compromise the indelible examples we are shown, tread a middle ground? That ground, we already suspected, was far shakier than acquiescence or rejection, the first act happening in an instant, the latter choice requiring a lifetime.

I hoped Dessa's shrug wasn't her instant, for I believed the world would have constant need of wonderful badness.

❀ ❀ ❀ ❀

Our friendship withered, no longer supple enough to withstand even minor debate, so when Dessa said I should invite Terrence to the Sadie Hawkins formal, I complied. She hinted we would have a great evening of it, that Terrence and her shot-putter (whom I knew in my mind as The Real Thing, Baby) were essential only to admit us at the auditorium door.

Terrence, too, fell into a dazed compliance from which he didn't recover until his public escort duty was done. "This isn't at all like you, Phoebe," he said, blinking absently when I asked him. "Does this mean I have to wear a suit?"

My mother, once again ablaze with usefulness, wanted a visual record of this night for my father, who was in Fresno chairing a symposium on self-fulfillment. She'd sewn me a puffed-sleeved gown, yellow voile flocked with daisies, lined with a satiny sheath. She took up the front of my hair, made a cluster of ringlets with the curling iron, and pushed daisies through the curls, her metallic breath singeing my face.

"You're gorgeous," she pronounced, stepping back with the camera.

I looked like an ornate table setting to which Terrence added a rosebud wrist corsage. "This really isn't like you," he said, cheeks flushed from nerves and aftershave.

"I know," I said. My mother snapped a picture while Terrence and I scrutinized the corsage as if it were about to take root in my arm.

At the dance, Terrence examined the decorated walls, panels of chicken wire stuffed with a rushed mosaic of crepe and tissue paper in Easter basket colors. "They could've at least painted a mural," he said, and Dessa appeared in a low-cut black mini, on the arm of The Real Thing, Baby.

"How darling you look, Phoebe," she purred. "Don't let your daisies wilt." Then she sauntered off to the dance floor.

"She's not at all like you, either," Terrence said. "Not even like herself. What is happening tonight?"

I wasn't sure. But everyone there—the athletes, the scholars, the long-haired dissidents, the slick-haired lowriders, and those who quietly awaited their identities—seemed cowed by the sameness of attire, like pets, scrubbed and beribboned, just released from a grooming salon.

Terrence and I danced, mainly the slow numbers, and felt good cleaving to each other, inhaling our own odors underneath the perfumed similarity. As we shuffled in circles, I kept watch for Dessa, who, contrary to her pre-dance intimations, avoided me all evening. Occasionally I glimpsed her back, or the froth of her hair in strobe light, but when she rotated behind her partner, his huge shoulders engulfed her and she disappeared from my view, like a child behind the trunk of a tree.

Between dances, Terrence and I had our paid-for photograph taken beside a potted juniper bush. "Say, 'Grief,'" the photographer playfully instructed, his head under a black cloth. "Makes for a nice, natural picture." He recited variations of this joke for every couple.

For a while, we amused ourselves at the refreshment table.

"Is this punch at all like me?" I said, holding a plastic cup in front of Terrence's nose.

"Is this miniaturized sandwich at all like me?" he said, brandishing a white bread triangle.

We kept on, intermittently, with the shamrock cookies, pastel mints, doughnuts, peanut butter celery, and even the doilies until Terrence said, "I don't think I can stand much more of this hilarity," and we left. I waved to Dessa, or rather in the direction of where I knew her to be.

❀ ❀ ❀ ❀

Terrence had a pint of blackberry brandy stashed in his mother's glove compartment. I imagined his father, the coach, slipped it to him on his way out the door, accompanied by a wink and an elbow nudge to the ribs, but I didn't question him. I remarked, as he drew the bottle from the compartment, that I'd been getting stoned for over three years, yet had never once been drunk.

"Then this isn't at all like you, either," he said, depositing the bottle in my lap, "and goes with the theme of the evening."

We parked at the tag end of Wells Drive, a lonely dirt road that ran alongside the NBC lot fence and stopped at Pacific Boys' Lodge, a group home for unadoptable teens. One of its occupants had a rift down the center of his forehead, from where his mother purportedly hit him with a hatchet when he was younger. There were horrible stories about what he'd done in retaliation, stories about the crimes and sorrows of other boys, too, that kept the deserted stretch of road from becoming a parking lot for lovers. Men didn't even walk their thigh-high watchdogs by the Boys' Lodge. I don't think they were so much afraid of the boys as they were bothered by the incursion of unwanted children in the very suburban neighborhoods dedicated to what was best for the young.

I took a swig of the brandy, passed it to Terrence, and leaned back in the seat to await its effect, an almost instant warmth emanating from my stomach lining. After a few more swallows, the warmth hit my brain. Unlike dope, which produced in me a cool, detached amusement, this stuff made my thought process fluid and jaunty. I shifted and stretched in the bucket seat.

"Yes?" Terrence said.

"Let's run," I said. I kicked off my yellow-tinted pumps, hiked up my flowery gown, and headed for the hole cut into the chain-link fence.

NBC had used the lot to film a few episodes of *Bonanza*, then let the acreage sit, a chaparral preserve in the midst of tract homes. Terrence and I ran down a rutted path through foxtails whitened by the milky light of a cloud-covered moon. The path veered to the right and entered an undulation of hills laden with mustard and thistle and scrub oak. At the base of a hill, we paused to gaze at intriguing litter, several sheets of green-and-ochre-painted plywood that during filming had camouflaged a decaying convertible Chevy. The car was now in plain view, a jimson weed growing through the rusted floorboard.

"There's your mural, Terrence," I said, unzipping my dress. "Let the real dance begin!"

"It is beautiful out here," he said, his lashes luminescent when he faced into the moonlight. "It would be a shame to waste beauty like this."

I ripped my fake lashes off, tossing them onto the ground where they looked, in the moon haze, like a pair of woolly bear caterpillars. Terrence kissed me, and we lay down on the silvery dirt and kissed more and harder. I was glad we were not in his mother's car, not in my parents' home, not on their carpet, not on any carpet at all. Then I felt the power of admitting and holding someone in me, of giving and receiving pleasure that evoked foreign sounds from our throats. And also the power of liquor, the lightheaded courage it gave me to be naked in the semi-dark of the open air.

Afterward, I wondered how Terrence and I, so complete and dazzling in our union, could seem so separate and ordinary lying side by side staring up at the sky. Terrence tried to push my dress underneath me as a mattress—I later hid the soiled dress in a paper bag in my closet—but I scooted it away, preferring the cold hard adobe at my back.

Even now, approaching forty, I think love is a tension between fear and knowledge, pain and comfort; the tension is akin to wonder and slackens as it's domesticated. I haven't married. Colleagues accept this information with the benign, tolerant smiles of academic professionals, but I see them recoil inwardly. At some later date, a woman will warn me of what I stand to miss by remaining childless, or a man will offer himself, misreading my childlessness for sexual need or inactivity. Actually, I find far more terrifying than biological deprivation the idea of enacting my adult life in the presence of a child both vulnerable and probing as my brother. My parents bravely saw the delusion of their marriage through till Pierce was in college, when they began a divorce that isn't over after fifteen years of litigation. Their lawyers afford them a ferocious avenue of communication they missed out on in their term as a couple. My cynicism about love, then, is tempered by my belief that we all ultimately get what we once sorely lacked.

In memory, my family thrives.

❁ ❁ ❁ ❁

Tuesday, my father returned from the Fresno symposium, and Tuesday night, the paper bag containing my homemade dress greeted me on my dinner plate. For a second, I couldn't identify it and unfurled the paper to look in. Pierce regarded the bag and me with a stoned interest I recognized as an avowal to live, and I grinned before I could stop myself.

"Amused?" my father said. "Suppose you explain the joke to me. Your mother spent fifty dollars and nearly as many hours putting that outfit together. How come it looks like you buried it and dug it up like a dog does a bone?"

"Why, that's exactly what happened, Dad," I said. "The full moon made me do it." I turned again to Pierce, refolded the bag, and didn't see my father's palm swipe at the side of my head.

He grasped the collar of my blouse like a drawer handle and pulled me toward him. "You watch your freewheeling mouth when you're at this table, young lady." I noticed the pulse at the side of his neck and forehead, his dark hair receding in coves. "You remember who you're talking to."

"I know who you are," I said, raising my chin at him. "Trust me."

My mother's lighter snapped brightly at the end of one of her cigarettes.

"Not now, Sandra," my father said. "There's enough bad air in this room already."

She lit the cigarette anyway, shot him a dour look while his face hardened with resignation. He released me. The expressions my parents wore were insular as the home they contrived, and I had to marvel at their capacity, at the human capacity, to adapt.

Pierce performed fervent origami on his paper napkin, a pair of disembodied wings. "Which came first?" he rasped, piloting the angular shape through the air before him. "The rare flying chicken, or the common egg?" and he wadded the napkin in his hand.

THE CURSE OF AMBROSIA

Outlaws, like poets, rearrange the nightmare.
—Tom Robbins

PROLOGUE: THE CURSE

I SIT ON THE SCALDING leather of our Lincoln Continental, rocking from one half of my butt to the other till each adjusts to the heat. My mother trots out a punchbowl of fruit salad for me to hold on our trip to church. I feel important in this duty, first of all because I love the stuff—marshmallows, oranges, pineapple chunks, sour cream, and coconut, folded up in a dessert she only makes when she wants to impress the church women—and secondly because my friend Phoebe is joining us, but she won't be the one holding the bowl.

Her mother the model has put her in a navy blue dress with a huge white collar, big as a toilet seat cover folded in half, and a red straw headband with netting. Phoebe has tiny dots of sweat on her nose and upper lip; I think she looks both pretty and ridiculous in her getup. I wear my usual white pleated skirt with the chocolate stain at the hem, and the only blouse I could find that was ironed. As part of my summer tradition, I've successfully hidden most of my dress clothes under my bed and at the bottom of my doll chest. Of course, on my head, I have the obligatory lace mantilla my mother thinks is part of the Catholic uniform. She converted in order to marry Daddy Otto. I'm supposed to call him Daddy, but in my mind he's Daddy Otto.

With the ambrosia and a promise that I could bring a friend, my mother bribed me into going to this church social. Daddy Otto is the only true Catholic in the picture, but he never attends church or anything to do with it.

"It's hotter than Hell's hot dog stand," I say to Phoebe as we wait. My butt has finally adjusted, and I'm thankful, for once, for the added protection of underwear. Usually it just seems pointless. I flick a mosquito bite on her leg.

She says, "Hotter than athlete's foot in Africa."

We giggle and snort and roll our eyes, until my mother arrives at the car, putting a towel across my skirt and the bowl in my lap.

"Hang on to it for dear life, Dessa, my darling," she says. "The ladies of Saint Mel's are depending on you." The tin foil is loose so I crimp it tighter, and we're off to the Summer Faith Spectacular. Try saying that with a mouthful of milky fruit.

❀ ❀ ❀ ❀

I see the lunatic suitor before my mother or Phoebe. Actually, I see him in my mind before I see him with my sight. What my mind shows me is not really him, but a warning of him, somehow: a slow motion film of the Rose Parade, which I am forced to watch with Daddy Otto every year on January first, while eating what he calls his "famous flapjacks." There is nothing famous about them; they're just regular pancakes made from Bisquick and water.

I've experienced warnings like this before, but they usually happen in dreams. Once, I dreamed an entire night of tornadoes, and when I picked up the newspaper in the morning, opening it before Daddy Otto just to see how much it would annoy him, the front page photos were ruined midwestern towns and funnel-shaped monsters like those in my nightmare. And we live in California. Tornadoes are as rare here as Indian-head nickels or icebergs.

"Mom!" I say, as she steers the car around a corner, and

there he is, only you can't really tell he's a man. He looks like a bouquet of four dozen red roses scurrying on two skinny pant legs, and he's no more than a couple of car lengths in front of us. "Mom, stop!"

She stomps the brake pedal as if it were vermin, the tires shriek, and everything tumbles forward: me, my friend, our hats, the bowl, and even one of Phoebe's patent leather flats ends up in the grit and carpet fuzz mixed with the ambrosia. Phoebe has a stray glob of it on her platter collar, and I look like I've used it as a skin treatment. We're stunned, and unroll like pill bugs from beneath the dashboard.

"God damn-o-rama city," my mother says. When she uses foul language she makes embarrassing attempts to disguise it. "Are you girls okay? Let's see your little faces, front and center," and she checks us for blood and breakage. "Hands and fingers?" she says, swiping at me with the towel, but I know we're okay. I know because Phoebe is doing her best to not burst into hysterical laughter, which fuels itself like atoms in the hydrogen bomb we've heard so much about.

To avoid my own urge to laugh, I peer out the window at the man behind the flowers, the cause of this mishap who's now made it to the sidewalk but is still not showing himself. I think he might be able to see us between the leaves and stems, though he remains faceless to me. I cock my head at him.

"Gotta go," he says, backing toward an apartment complex. "I'm gonna propose, if it's all right with you." And just like that, he reaches sideways for a familiar latch, and disappears behind a wooden gate.

My mother gazes after him, her mouth hanging open like something mechanical that's stuck. Finally, she murmurs, "May your children be in diapers till they're dating." She leans back in the driver's seat and exhales a colossal sigh, massaging her abdomen. Her linen sheath stretches so tight over it I can see the stitched outline of her girdle's control panel.

"Fudge sticks," she says, with a kind of tremor in her voice. "To top it all off, I've got The Curse."

Phoebe and I are old enough to know what The Curse is, yet, ever since that day, I've taken my mother's meaning as this: whenever a bowl is chock full of something delicious, something you love, it is also doomed to be dumped and lost before it can be savored.

I write this for Theo, so he knows.

Eggs in Viable Shells

It began with the first dolphin, dead from algae bloom, washing up on the Balboa Peninsula.

It began with sewage systems.

It began when a guy named Benz got the brilliant idea to power a carriage with an internal combustion engine.

It began with gunpowder, or maybe hairspray.

It began with life forms we didn't recognize but helped create.

It began with hurricanes, quakes, blizzards, droughts, floods, tsunamis, tornadoes, and more so-called natural disasters than we could keep up with.

It began as a strange odor, like burning sugar and shoe rubber, we noticed at first then got used to.

It began as dogs and prophets howled mournfully, and we laughed at them.

It began as smoke that stung the eyes but made for beautiful sunsets.

It began when someone paired intelligence with permission to destroy.

Somewhere in all this, it began, the end did. And one afternoon, right around the time I realized I would live to see the end, my friend Phoebe Dunn, after close to seventy years of absence, came back into my life, and we started the doctrine of Might As Well.

❈ ❈ ❈ ❈

Of course, I didn't recognize her at first. We'd been in a strangled knot of people, had ducked and wiggled our way to the start of it, and were wearing our Enviromasks for the quick exit we'd each planned. Phoebe's mask was a caramel color that blended with her face, mine a bright violet. I figured if we had to wear these contraptions to survive, they might as well be obvious. No matter what color they were, though, the masks almost completely obscured faces. All but the eyes.

Phoebe and I reached for the same two cartons of eggs at the same time, the last two. Some rancher close by had managed to shelter his chickens enough to keep them laying eggs with actual shells instead of fragile, mushy membranes. Most eggs were sold in cartons, like milk, or in fake plastic shells similar to those filled with jellybeans and hidden at Easter egg hunts. The real thing, eggs in viable shells, was cause for near riot at the supermarket, and Phoebe and I, by virtue of the invisibility of advanced age, had managed to finagle our way to the forefront of the mob.

These are the first words I said to my old friend: "Let go of the eggs, ancient bitch, or I'll rip your wig off." I was hoping intimidation would work and I could slink out of the crowd as invisibly as I slunk in, twenty-four eggs richer.

But Phoebe was Phoebe, and if she didn't recognize me, she recognized my style. "How about we share them, like sweet old-fashioned grannies, and leave these people in shock?"

Which is exactly what we did, toddling away with our arms around each other's waists, out through the scanner that read our Magnabags, into the boiling haze of day.

When we began to laugh, halfway down the street, she had trouble stopping, and that, combined with her peering dark eyes, was how I knew it was Phoebe Dunn.

She invited me to her place for an omelet. "I have some dried avocado just for the occasion," she said. Avocados were a junk food invented in heaven: bright yellow-green and smooth inside a bumpy exterior, so buttery and rich it was hard to believe they were good for you. No matter how firm they were when picked, they wouldn't keep longer than a day anymore, so were immediately sliced, freeze-dried and sold far cheaper than the fresh specimens.

Lettuce or any crisp vegetable was a wilted thing of the past.

It had been a while since I shared a home cooked meal at a friend's place, and we had decades of blanks to fill in about each other. So, despite her nabbing a carton of gourmet eggs I might have made off with myself at the Superplex, I joined her.

❀ ❀ ❀

I kept Phoebe talking.

I didn't want to tell her about my two divorces yet, or why I lived in a room with a shared bath, rather than having an entire floor to myself, as she did. That what I settled on from my ex-husbands was mostly dependent on social security, and, well, pamphlets and pundits try to explain how that fairy tale ended. I stashed away enough to survive on, as long as I didn't live past ninety. That was one good thing about the end—it lightened my financial worries. And if I did live longer than anticipated, I fantasized about joining the Dot Robber and his merry band of rebels. Do something good for humanity, such as it was.

I didn't want to speak of my gift, either, though whether I mentioned it or not, it always affected my relationships. I tried to ignore it when I was a teenager, forcibly forgetting my dreams and acting oblivious with friends, but, like most things we ignore, it came back stronger and with vengeance.

Since Phoebe had been a teacher, a social anthropologist, and paid into a state retirement system, and since she'd never married, she had more to live on than I, who'd married two millionaires. I was the reason they'd made their money, investors and my gift, you see, but my gift could not be classified a profession on any tax form. And men are excellent at forgetting during divorces all the help that gifted women were to them, and men are also talented at burying money, the way squirrels bury acorns and rake leaves back over the spot for extra protection.

Phoebe had made a living studying happiness. "A barren area in anthropology," she said. "Happiness mystified me. I thought if I studied it, I could bring it closer."

I didn't tell her the day her younger brother tried to hang himself all those decades ago, I'd known it would happen. Or that the reason I threw up was not because I'd seen Pierce dangling by a dog leash, but because I'd noticed the leash the day before in the Dunns' garage and imagined blood on it. He'd always been a strange kid, yet no one could've seen that coming without, well, without outside help.

"Do you have any children?" I asked her.

"Never married," she said, and set the omelet, steaming, on the table. She began to slice it, carefully as a holiday roast.

"That never stopped a gal from having children."

"Didn't actually stop me either. The drug my mother took when she was pregnant with me did, however. Another egg problem."

I didn't tell her about the child I gave birth to, prematurely, probably because of the abortions I had in the '70s combined with the drugs I took. The child I held in my arms till he died, the child I named and buried in a tiny white casket. Whose death depressed me so much my second husband divorced me, saying, "Jesus, Dessa, snap out of it. I married you because you knew how to play."

I forgot how.

"What have you learned about happiness?" I asked her.

I listened as she explained how we North Americans had it all wrong, that being an individual, establishing yourself as *someone,* was not the key, as we'd seen time and again with the divorce and suicide rates of celebrities. Balinese culture, for example, discouraged individuality. In fact, children were given the same names, regardless of gender, according to their birth order: Wayan, Made, Nyoman, etc. The people of Bali had little money, and hence no financial worries. Few had any delusions of getting ahead. They ate simple and mostly fresh foods, and created beauty wherever they could with offerings of fruit and flowers and incense at Hindu altars, so numerous you had to step around them on sidewalks. Happiness was theirs until the waves leveled many islands of Indonesia. That was when Phoebe retired from academia.

"Still close to your family?" I asked, before she could ask me anything.

"Pierce. Every so often. His wife keeps him on a tether, and needs to. He drinks like a lord. My parents are gone, of course. Slugged it out in court till he had a heart attack and she inoperable cancer of the pancreas." Phoebe took a few more bites, chewing slowly, and stared out the window. "The poor pathetic dears loved each other that much." She studied another bite of reconstituted avocado she was about to take. "And your folks?"

Oh, she was clever. Start with my parents, then sashay onto the topic of me.

"Dead, both of them. Lung and heart disease, and one within a year of the other."

"Yes," she said, nodding. "If cigs and liquor didn't get them, the environment did. The world went from boundless to spent in their lifetime, or thereabouts. We're the ragged end of it. I marvel every day that I'm still here."

The omelet was so delicious, spongy, and rich, that I chewed for a period of time without speaking. My eyes were open, but pictures started forming in my mind, nonsensical at first, roads and trees and stones, dirt and traffic signs and blankets blowing by me like a storm, then the images settled into steadiness. I saw a long line of men in dark suits, among them one who was naked, a splotch of pink in all the sameness.

"Ever fall in love?" I asked her.

Phoebe dabbed at her mouth with a dishcloth. "Truly, deeply, and inappropriately. He was married. I lied to myself and to him when I said I could bear it."

"Bear what?" I said. "The competition?"

"No. I didn't want all his time and attention. It was my own yearning I couldn't put up with."

I must have looked confused or interested, because she continued. "Crept over me like sickness. When I was with him, I was so depleted by the yearning, I had no energy for him, the object of it all. I mean, essentially I curled up next to him like a cat who wanted to be stroked. Not like anything human."

"Dramatic ending?" I asked. I slid another hunk of omelet onto my plate.

"Hardly," she said. "An airport. A goodbye I didn't realize was the last. A cliché."

"Rain or fog involved?"

"No, thankfully."

When I married, both times, it was simple: I assumed he would take care of me and I would take care of him. It worked out that way for a while, then we parted. Not much yearning involved, except at the very beginning, and it disappeared like smoke, showing us the truth of our common arrangement. I'd wondered what it was like to be madly in love, even as a girl. My relationships always seemed like something expected rather than something that took me by surprise.

"Dess?"

"Uh huh?" I thought she'd bombard me with all the questions I hoped to sidestep.

"Listen," she said, and busied herself with a bottle of wine she was attempting to uncork. "I hope this isn't vinegar. I never drink alone, and consequently, hardly ever drink."

Avocado *and* wine, I thought. Life is good tonight.

We clinked glasses. "To old friends," she said. "Very fucking old. Incidentally, this isn't a wig. I've managed to retain my hair, not to mention a few of my teeth."

"Cheers," I said. "Sorry. My mistake." Her hair was arranged in such a thick white puff of a pageboy that it really did look fake. I was still tempted to try to pull it off her but restrained myself. What little hair I have I keep cut in short wisps under a baseball cap when I'm indoors and without a hood.

"Dess?"

Okay. Here came the questions. I slugged back my entire glass of zinfandel, in case I had to leave quickly. I could always say I didn't feel well from the food. Usually, I ate from packages and cans.

"How shall I say this? I worked hard as a public servant, but I know what happened in the private sector. You see what I have here." Her age-mottled hand swept the air to the left and right of her.

"You want a round of applause?" Why was she lording this over me? It wasn't like Phoebe Dunn to brag. Was this some reckoning for the tricks I played on her as a child? All the challenges I won, boys I dated? Was she giving me a sunset nanny-nanny-nanner? I looked around, and the place wasn't so fabulous: two bedrooms and a bath down the hall, worn bamboo floors, large living and dining area and respectable kitchen, all painted a soothing beige, so soothing it irritated me. A butter-colored leather couch with at least a decade of use. Lots of painted-bark and beaded leather artifacts from her travels. Dingy window blinds. "Let's give a big cheer for public service," I said.

"Shit," Phoebe said. Her face drooped like old ladies' socks. Like our socks. "I didn't mean for it to sound so self-congratulatory. What I meant to do was ask if you want to stay here. Indefinitely. Move all your belongings in if you'd like. I'll give you the room I used as a study. There's nothing really to study anymore, short of how the planet's dying, and I'm as bored with that topic as everyone else."

If her face had drooped, mine must have stood at attention. "What?" I said. Kindness and generosity were not in abundance these days as people struggled to survive, as if we weren't all going to perish by the same sunspot licking into the atmosphere, or wall of water, or hail of cosmic garbage, or viral plague, or tide of irradiated sludge, or explosion meant to teach a lesson we already knew too well. As if one of us might somehow outrun what was coming for us. Before she died, my mother said the struggle was because of hope, and I said it was because of stupidity. They might be two sides of the same attitude.

Phoebe remained silent. This was worse than if she'd at that moment asked me about marriage and children.

"Are you serious?" I continued, and she looked at me like a subject in one of her happiness studies. "I'm not homeless, you know. I have a place in the Apartments Formerly Called the Promenade. There are lofts. It's a swanky joint." It was swanky if you were lucky enough to have a loft, only I had a studio with a shared bathroom from which I often had to scrub a stranger's filth, or else sit on it.

"Dessa, I know you're not homeless. You're nothing like homeless. I was asking for selfish reasons. We could keep each other company, play cards, share meals, wait for the inevitable together. Maybe get into some trouble like we did as girls. Why not? There's not even a future to leave as a legacy." Her voice was quavery with contained emotion, maybe even embarrassment. I knew she was serious.

"How long do I have to think about it?" I said.

"Long as you want. Take your time." She poured more wine in my empty glass and took a seat again.

"What kind of trouble were you thinking about?"

"Anything our impaired brain cells can come up with." My friend looked up from her lap and grinned.

❀ ❀ ❀ ❀

I Dot-messaged her two days later, after a vision I tried my best not to have.

I'd watched movies on the wall monitor, old mindless movies about adventure and plunder that glossed over what such pursuits really led to. Then, when my Per Diem Energy Cache expired, I sat in the suddenly quiet room, looking out the glass block window that distorted everything I might have been able to witness outside, and it was just as well. The blur of a passing HoverBug, or the metallic bundle of a mid-air collision (and what was left of the people in it) sinking to the ground under a forlorn rag of white emergency chute. Smoke in an array of greys, yellows, and beiges. Angry exclamations muffled by masks, or listless eyes with nothing left to say.

I thought of the loneliness I felt, now that I had been offered an alternative. Before, I hadn't realized I was lonely; I had just spent my days as if they were in endless supply.

My message to Phoebe read: *Hw mch r u askn fr rnt?*

She Dotted back immediately, which told me she'd been waiting, and I read as the letters crawled across the ovoid screen stretched into the web of skin between my thumb and forefinger: *Nt mch. A thsnd inclds evrthng.*

That was less than half of what I paid for a cramped hovel whose corners had so many layers of grunge it was part of the building's structural integrity. Still, I didn't want to seem too desperate. *Mght as wll,* I Dotted.

My vision was something clearer than what showed through my window, though not completely formed. In it, an orange glow illuminated skin and sand and water. A palm tree burned, but the flames were shaped like the fronds, almost as if the fire grew slowly on its subjects rather than attacking them. Around me were many, many people, some I sensed I knew and some I didn't. The only one I recognized was by the puff of her white hair taking on the orange.

Ys. Mght as wll, she Dotted back.

Live Ones

WHAT HAD I GOTTEN MYSELF into?

Moving from solitude to built-in companionship overnight was like waking from a state of sleep and finding myself in the middle of a Dot Robber fantasy that was not as heroic as I'd imagined. The Dot Robber was equal parts real person and urban mythological savior who supposedly worked in the night and delivered government prisoners from their worse-than-average hell to freedom and anonymity, all by surgically removing their Dot devices. I wanted to believe in him (or her) in the same way I wanted to believe my new life with Phoebe was a positive move. Let's just say it took me a while to adjust, and I was sometimes cross with Phoebe when I had no legitimate cause to be—when she'd laugh at a passage in one of her beloved books she was memorizing for the umpteenth time, for example, or when she asked me if I wanted rye toast, as if it were a delicacy whose appeal was born again each morning. Or when she stared, slack-jawed, at the news we watched on the monitor wall, and her head bobbed down and up in a prelude to sleep. We had blocked out times to use our Per Diem Energy Cache for the floor we occupied, times when the monitor was hers, times when it was mine, and times when we watched together. Our PDEC was far more than the allotment I'd had in my single room. Still, I begrudged her the time she had control of it. I had to pause and remind myself, *Dessa, you agreed to this*, yet often I was overcome with resentment to the point that I'd banish myself to my room. There I sat with my Hawaiian-style furniture, too tropical to blend with her Danish Modern pieces throughout the rest of our living space, and stared out the window my eyes could actually see through. I confess I even resented not being blind anymore to the outside world, and turned away from the haze that seldom cleared and the people who were far less lucky than I was in their living arrangements. Some of them slept on the damp concrete of public bathrooms. There was a recent court case involving a man who sued LA County, claiming to have been misled by official signs that directed him to *restrooms*. Shortly thereafter, new signs were stamped out pointing the way to public *lavatories*.

I planned to move again as soon as I found a studio with a private bath. In dreaming of this escape from companionship, I calmed down enough to accept it. Maybe that's how we learn to live with anything—by plotting a way out, and day after day deciding to stay put.

Besides, the move was not without benefit.

I loved leaving the decades of congealed grime and sorting through the garbage of my life. I left a note for my unseen bathroom mate: "Hey, Big Guy, please learn to clean up after yourself so the next person doesn't gag on your messes. Who toilet trained you—a wooly mammoth?" I disposed of divorce papers governing agencies cared nothing about, having more pressing concerns on their dockets and time working against them; I threw out photographs no one would be left to care about, keeping only a few I might want to pore over to remind myself of wedding days, birthday parties, vacations at lost and lovely places. Key West. Kauai. Bimini. Apollonia on the island of Sifnos. Venice. I tossed cards and letters from people I had forgotten or wanted to forget, but kept those that reminded me I'd lived a life. I sensed every now and then I'd need to assure myself of that.

I saved the receiving blanket I'd wrapped my son in, Theodore Hauser Daly, small and slim as an evening purse, and the hat and booties I'd knitted him. I felt duty-bound to keep them, since he would never grow into them. I'm not sure about the logic in that reasoning, but there it was. The blanket had long since lost his sweet, temporary smell, but at times I could almost conjure it.

❀ ❀ ❀

I knew I would stay after I told Phoebe about Theo.

She didn't coax the story out of me; it was in me, waiting to be delivered just as he had been: painfully and with little hope. I was barely at twenty-three weeks when the contractions came in earnest.

I simply started talking one night when Phoebe and I headed to our rooms for sleep, after the late night comedy newscast we preferred to the actual news. People had been doing this for years, substituting entertainment for fact. Nothing could be made of real knowledge anyway, since even our votes had stopped being more than metaphor, like saluting the flag, or burning it.

Phoebe trundled down the hall, singing, "Time to say goodnight, gooooood-night, gooooood-night," which she did as habitually as she ate rye toast, but what I said stopped her before she disappeared behind her door.

"I had a child once. Not a stillborn, not a miscarriage—a live birth that didn't last much longer than thoughts I have these days."

Her heavy-lidded eyes stretched open. "Want to talk about it, Dess?"

"Why do you think I mentioned it?" I said this with a nasty edge, as though she were responsible for the whole ordeal. It was almost as if I wanted to punish her with my story because she'd been so kind to me. We humans, as a species, are prone to lash out at kindness and cower at cruelty. Not our finest tendency.

It all came burbling out of me, though: I hadn't really

wanted a child at forty-one, although lots of other women of our era were having babies later in life with great joy and anticipation, and my husband, Jerry, was thrilled. He'd said, *I'm still shooting live ones*, and took me out dancing at the Hyatt Newporter, before it got turned into apartments. (All habitable space was now apartments—that, or Distress Centers for the destitute and homeless.) But I didn't eat well, didn't take in enough fruits and vegetables and proteins, and succumbed to my cravings for ice cream—which did have calcium in it, after all—and shave ice, popsicles, anything cold because the hormonal surges caused me to sweat all the time. I was not a radiant pregnant woman. I didn't glow, except for the hot flashes. I especially didn't like the way my aging belly skin—damaged from years of being a sun goddess in southern California—started to stretch like the leather of an old satchel. (*Remember the lengths we went to to fry ourselves, Phoebe?* I asked, and she nodded, pulling at the crepey skin on her forearm.) I slathered on the cocoa butter as an antidote to stretch marks, and when we'd go out for dinner and drinks with friends, they ordered tropical cocktails, even in February, because the smell was so suggestive, and I sipped on a sparkling water with lemon, feeling like a big bulging scratch 'n' sniff sticker.

Jerry was the one who glowed, really. I sat around reading trashy tabloids or knitting. Couldn't possibly concentrate on anything else, with the flashes, and my feet up on the coffee table because my ankles were as big around as orchid pots. It was the only time he waited on me, popsicle after popsicle. Orange was my favorite. I tried not to think about the two years of stinky diapers I had ahead of me.

I went into early labor, and they could tell this baby was coming at the hospital, coming fast. The pain was unbelievably awful, so intense I bellowed, and though he was barely a pound, he might as well have been full term. The minute I caught sight of him, so tiny and perfect on the outside, I couldn't imagine not wanting him. I wanted him more than anything I'd ever wanted in my entire life, more than money, or to be loved for my true self, or world peace. I wanted that little purplish person. They rushed him out of the room, and Jerry followed. After what seemed like only a few minutes but was really more than an hour, I guess, Jerry came back. His mask was off. My regular doctor was gone, too, and there was a neo-natal specialist in front of me, saying, *We're sorry, it's untenable*, and I said, *What? What's untenable? Be specific.* He said, *Your baby's survival. Intestinal malformation, lungs won't respond to treatment. We can keep him alive on machines he'll need for the rest of his life, or you can hold him until he passes.*

I held him. I held Theo, wrapped in a blanket he didn't really need to keep him warm because he would never have a chance to get sick. His head was the size of a tangerine. I held him until he stopped breathing, and then I kept holding him and wouldn't let anyone take him. I screamed and spit and threatened to kill anyone who touched him. I'm sure they sedated me because when I woke up, Theo was gone, and Jerry was looking at me with a stare as huge and blank as a blown wall monitor. A couple months later, he left me after I made a remark about his "live ones" not being lively as he'd thought.

❀ ❀ ❀ ❀

As I finished, Phoebe stood with her arms clutched to her torso, as if she were holding the child I'd just told her about, or maybe one she'd dreamed up herself. She wasn't crying. The premise of holding a dead baby goes beyond sadness, into a realm of emotion that's not suited to a single word, that a collection of words would trivialize.

When we were girls, I razzed Phoebe about her sensitivity, as afraid of it as I was my gift. I liked her for it now. Which is why I then told her that, several times during my unsuccessful pregnancy, I saw a vision of a small white shoebox next to a pile of dirt.

"I'm not sure I understand," she said, and dropped her arms. "Are you saying you caused his death with a recurring hallucination?"

"No," I said. "I knew he was going to die. I have these visions a lot. Have had them my entire life."

Many questions were in her stare, and I said, "Yeah, as a child I had them. When Pierce tried to hang himself on Volare's leash, after your folks gave the dog away? I knew that would happen. And I don't know if I threw up because I knew it, and saw it for real, or because I was relieved he was still alive, despite the vision."

She tilted her head and looked at me for a long time. Finally she said, "Jesus God, Dessa. What a burden you've borne. All that, and two husbands." She put her arms around me, even though my body was rigid with the shock of showing myself to someone, and I was still a good half-foot taller than she was. Our spines had shrunk at the same rate, I suppose. Her head bumped against my chin and clacked my teeth together, and suddenly we both began laughing, then the laughter turned to confused tears.

I said, "I think I tried *not* to love him. You know, because I knew he was going to die, I tried not to." I sobbed in giant howls I'd been saving up for who knows how many years, calendars full of howls, unwritten journals of them.

Phoebe walked me over to the couch, sat me down, and made some chamomile tea. She had tins of tea she stockpiled and used for specific events, like the hysterical, ranting revelations of old, childless women.

I emptied myself out. I reminded her of the ambrosia incident, and told her of how I'd helped my first husband make money in telecommunications just as the cell phone came into being. The vision I had was one that became normal for a long while, of thousands of people driving in cars, or jogging on the beach, or walking through malls in the same pose of elbow bent with hand at ear. And how I'd helped Jerry by dreaming a block of houses—shacks, really, pastel shacks—in Laguna Beach, and describing them to him because the image kept interrupting my dreams like breaking news. We cruised around Laguna one weekend to see if we could find them, and, "Bingo! Look," I said. "For sale, too." He bought the entire block for three-hundred grand, and within four years the property was worth close to six million. By then, he'd snapped up a few other beach shacks.

I told her I was relieved each husband I divorced, because I'd stopped being a person for either man, but was more their personal Geiger-counter for profit. I spent the settlements fast in travel. "Running away," I said. "An art I've perfected, except I've never gone far enough away from myself." I'd counted on their pensions to get me through old age.

I could tell Phoebe was tired; her eyes sagged and she did her characteristic head dip once in a while, but she stayed awake listening until 3:00 a.m. when I finally slowed like a runaway truck hitting a gravel ramp.

She didn't seem the least bit shocked, by the time we went to bed. "Let's sleep till lunchtime," she said. "It takes a lot of energy to be old."

When my empty body stretched out on the mattress, I felt like it was levitating. I thought, as I dozed off to the hum of my own snores and the drone of a distant Emergicopter, that the only thing better than friendship is a second chance at one.

Who Knew

I slept the sleep of a teenager and dreamed of trailing my arm through a koi pond. It resembled a pond at the house in Hanalei that Jerry and I owned, once upon a lifetime, only that one didn't have fish in it, just lilies. In my dream, the fish clustered around my skin and brushed their round mouths against me as if it were a form of worship.

I felt wonderful. Phoebe was there too, her hair still in the poofy pageboy, but it was as dark as when she was a girl. Everything else about her was old as her real age. She sat in a deck chair, peacefully reading; plumeria blossoms dropped into her hair and onto the pages of her book, and she'd sigh and brush them off.

Neither one of us wore an Enviromask or Envirobe in my dream of outdoors, nor did we worry about doing so.

I said to Phoebe, "You never told me about your true love. I'd like to hear that story."

She sighed again and brushed another blossom from her head. "For pity's sake, Dess. You really don't want to subject yourself to my nostalgia, do you?"

"Maybe," I said, not raising my eyes from the water.

She was quiet, and when I looked up, she had gone back

to her book. I didn't feel rebuffed by her. I continued to lounge in the sun, my submerged arm and a soft trade wind helping me maintain a comfy body temperature. I thought of how this setting, this situation, would have horrified us in adolescence—two old women doing nothing to speak of, and doing it without men—but how peaceful and satisfying it was now. The irony made me start to giggle, then wholeheartedly laugh.

"What's so funny?" Phoebe asked, and another plumeria flower plopped stem-first, dead center on her head. That she didn't realize it was sticking out of the very top of her seemed even funnier and kept me laughing.

"Okay, what's so funny?" she said, and I woke to Phoebe standing in my doorway, asking me the same question: "What's so funny?"

I rubbed my eyes to make sure she no longer had a pink plumeria bursting from her hair like a miniature propeller.

"A dream. Sorry," I sputtered. "Can't explain."

"Okay," she said, though my remark did not require agreement. "I know we were going to sleep in, but I've had a rather interesting chat."

I waited, still in dream fog.

Phoebe told me she'd just Screenfaced with a colleague from her years at Santa Monica College, Isabella Pugliese, an environmental specialist, Rank 5. "Bella keeps track of such things. There's a Clear Beach Day to be announced. Crystal Cove. We start now, we might gain admission, for a small fee. Imagine it, Dess—a beach day!"

I was half in my dream, the water a cool, clingy fabric on my arm, and I said, "Hmmmmm."

"What do you think?" she said, cheeks pink from the combination of rest and impatience.

I had no idea what route we would take, what transportation we would use. But in the afterglow of an evening at the koi pond, such pleasure seemed possible. I said, "Might as well," though, as my mind cleared I added, "How will we do this?"

From the Superplex to the Solarwear Outlet and Exchange Center, where we turned in our robes and masks to be recycled; to the Kioskbank, which replaced all larger banking buildings when they were converted to living spaces; to the Corner Cafe, which somehow never went out of style, Phoebe and I walked everywhere we went. Most people did, or rode a hooded personal transporter—HOPT, a kind of a cross between a scooter and a golf cart—but we didn't dare. Older citizens, such as ourselves, were prey to gangs of abandoned teenagers, some on skateboards, most with weapons, who would just as soon knock you off your HOPT and take it as they would shoot you, and we hoped never to be forced to choose either option.

Walking kept our bones healthy. There weren't many places to go, anyway. Live theatre had devolved into live rages and couplings or worse, and movies were simply a reflection of all that onscreen. Even if we'd found a movie worth seeing, who wanted to risk sitting for two hours with strangers in a dark, unguarded room? City parks were campgrounds for the homeless released from Distress Centers; libraries were museums since electronic publishing had its way with books of paper and cloth; art museums became the gated homes of the ultra-rich, who purchased them in the Great Collapse, and only invited their ultra-rich friends to visit.

Forget about hovercraft. By and large, the city's criminals and the law enforcement officers who chased them operated the flying death traps we saw out our fourth story windows. No one drove automobiles, not even hybrids, after gasoline ceased to be pumped at neighborhood stations, and was sold instead in half gallon cans at permit stores. A permit alone cost a year's rent; if any bold soul tried to bluff with a fake permit, two government guards would escort him, more or less intact, to the nearest Detention Center. Freeways broke apart like ancient pottery. Even so, they were traveled by Ecotrams powered by vegetable fuels, swerving left and right to avoid faults and potholes. The only other eco-fueled vehicles on the road were those whose owners had the parts and know-how to maintain them.

A wild ride to Crystal Cove on an Ecotram would cost us a half-month's rent.

How would we get there?

I narrowed my eyes at my friend, wondering if she'd lost her mind and I was being sucked into the vortex along with her. And what did she do? She grinned at me, and chirped orders. "Bring your SunSalve and wear your best undies. Nothing with rips or stains. I've got a secret weapon."

❀ ❀ ❀ ❀

The weapon, as she called it, was floors below in the underground parking garage I didn't know existed. Past the bicycles and transporters locked to metal bars, and the occasional hovercraft bin, past defunct Mercedes and Hondas and Volkswagens, was a locked cubicle to which Phoebe had the key, and in it was a bright red EV1.

"Purchased in 1997," she said. "For the new millennium. I balked at using it because they never quite caught on, and servicing was, well, difficult at best. I still try to take it out twice a year. I'm due. It'll be much safer with you as my passenger."

Phoebe had already begun to dust the electric car briskly with a cloth she'd dug out of the trunk. I said, "I thought all these were returned to their maker."

Her hair wobbled with her arm motions, which didn't stop as she spoke. "Clearly, not *all* of them. And stop dawdling. This vehicle's charged to the gonads."

When Phoebe used street slang, she did it with authority. Many former teachers, I'd noticed, retired with this talent, as if they reveled in the chance to say what they'd always wanted to say in the classroom. I did as I was commanded, the whole time singing in my head what was quickly becoming my mantra, "Might as well, might as well," the lazy tune given words by a band called The Grateful Dead.

❀ ❀ ❀ ❀

It was mid-September. The way you could know this, aside from looking at a calendar, was that the temperature was close to a hundred and twenty, and all plant life was crinkled and dry. The dryness worked in our favor because we planned to use Topanga Canyon to the coast. Seasons of fires had left the Santa Monica Mountains with sparse vegetation so that any rare measurable rainfall caused landslides and closed canyon routes for days at a time, or weeks. We had a clear shot if the car could hold a charge. Phoebe said it would get us there, though coming back might present a problem.

On our way out of Woodland Hills, teenage vagabonds, wearing cut-off robes over jeans and no hoods or masks, pelted the car with wet paper garbage and plastic containers they collected to make money. "Get that gas-sucking whore off the road," one of them yelled, his teeth brown with decay. I remembered the days when a good part of the California Dream focused on fluoride, orthodontia, and protest that made intellectual sense. No longer. Most of these teenvags, as we called them, were parentless, literally or figuratively, their folks dead from illness or the drugs they paradoxically needed to stay alive. Teenvags roamed the former suburban streets year round. I say *former* because who knew what to call any area now, with everything baking into the same dust? There weren't even public schools to contain these kids anymore, the campuses transformed to Distress Centers when the government gave education over to wall monitors. Yes, wall monitors. Homeschooling by technology. This didn't take a revolution. But gradually, it came to be that all teachers had to be on the same page of the same textbook series on the same day, and all students had to pass the same standardized tests, so the numbers crunchers—who never die, who will survive the last days of earth as efficiently as cockroaches—determined that the wall monitor would be the more cost-effective mode for education. Teachers were given golden, silver, bronze, and iron handshakes, and escorted off into retirement, no longer blamed for the ignorance of the masses. Wall monitors took on that responsibility.

The boy with the brown-veined teeth spat on the car's hood as the light changed. "Fucking old hags drivin' a hunk of Iranian gas-sucking shit."

I glanced at Phoebe, whose cheeks colored. In our girlhood, she might have ignored this teenvag moron, might have pitied him, but age had given her brassiness, a crazy kind of courage. I used to be one who called upon that quality, but something in life had leeched it from me, and now I rarely did.

Phoebe would retaliate.

She rolled the window down, the car out of the intersection, pulled her mask aside and shouted, "Does the word ELECTRIC mean anything to you, Fang Boy? Look it up in the dictionary, if you know what *that* is."

She pursed her lips primly, replaced the mask, and drove on, which was when I began to laugh so hard my lungs hurt. "Fang Boy?" I said. "Oh my God, Phoebe. That was classic. Vintage. Flash of brilliance."

She smiled with her eyes. "You think?" she said.

I wondered how any man could love and leave her. I wondered how any man could leave either of us. But most of them were dead now, anyway.

❈ ❈ ❈ ❈

The EV1 hummed along the canyon road. Phoebe explained an anonymous donor left the car to the college for exhibition, and when it ceased to be an asset or a draw, the foundation sold it to her for the cost of a few extra batteries. She drove it every now and then to keep it operable, and friends from the vocational ed. department tweaked it when she had a problem. Until the college shut down, of course. Now she was on her own.

There were numerous potholes, and bites of outer asphalt had tumbled into ravines, but it was mostly safe and even travel. Topanga Canyon was a place altered from what I knew in my teens and twenties, when it was a haven for hippies and rock stars and every bean curd or drug cult imaginable. Housing developments were built from the '70s into the new millennium, though the tract homes now stood abandoned, chimneys toppled from earthquakes, some charred from fire, others graffitied. The village and its craft centers where I once shopped for hand-tooled purses were gone or boarded up; I saw a cadaverous dog lift its leg on an empty redwood planter. The people who remained here lived in cabins and caves. They weren't hippies anymore but survivalists, and you didn't want to mess with them, so I'd heard.

Neither of us commented on the fallow place that had been a vibrant region of our teen lives. In our senior year, Phoebe and I secretly attended a party in the Canyon, telling our parents we were going to watch debate team practice, though neither of us cared a bit about debating. At the party, I sat next to a guy who seemed paunchy and glazed the whole while he blathered at me about fake hippies, until someone handed him a guitar. When he sang a line from "Rock and Roll Woman," I realized he was Stephen Stills. Phoebe and I laughed so hard over this we almost drove her mother's station wagon over Topanga Canyon's edge on the way home, but when you're young, close calls are comedy rather than warning. They are tales to tell. They're not the constant nearness of death we humans are pathetically good at ignoring.

I remembered we'd concocted another lie—God only knows what—so we could ditch school and drive through another canyon—Malibu—to witness the Pink Lady before she was obliterated by gallons of beige paint and lost to legend. Craning our necks for an hour, we gawked at the gorgeous, naked brunette, clutching a bouquet, stories above the Malibu tunnel, and thought out loud about the intriguing man who'd given her life on the sheer rock face. It had to have been a man who painted a naked woman. Had to. Months later, we learned a woman had created her, a secretary from Northridge, dangling from a rope scaffold one moon-bathed night until her project was complete.

Those were hopeful and heady times, over before we knew what could be done with them. Nothing that followed held the potential we squandered.

Phoebe and I were alone in our reverent thoughts of canyon places, till I broke the silence with a feeble joke. "Will there be a lifeguard to ogle?" I said, elbowing her.

"Doubtful," Phoebe said. "State's bankrupt, and the federal

monitor zombies don't lose two snores of sleep over drowning victims." She checked her mirrors cautiously, though we'd seen maybe four personal transporters the whole trip. "And if they're washed out to sea, voila. No burial costs."

I said, "Hmmm. I can throw away my Last Day Kit and wade out in the water. Hooray for me."

She pulled the wheel sharply to the left to avoid a fallen seagull. They did that with frequency these days, just fell from the sky, their light bodies defenseless to super-heated poisons.

"Dess," Phoebe said. "We may have some company. Bella will be there. Oh, and Terrence—you know, Terrence, my high school flame?"

I saw, in my mind, an image of the boy as a candle with a flame for a head. He actually had been tall and thin as a candle, and I smiled at the picture I'd made of the gawky boy and the *old flame* expression. "Oh, yes," I said. "I remember, all right." She'd thought he was God's gift, and I told her he was about as sexy as a circus geek on stilts, back when I believed sexiness was what made for lasting love.

"You never thought much of Terrence, did you?" She stopped the car delicately at the Coast Highway signal, which was missing its yellow light, but appeared to be otherwise functional.

Something in her tone, some sense of privilege to pry for information that might displease her, angered me, and I shot back, "Don't think we're best friends again. Don't think everything is peachy dandy because I told you about my dead baby last night, got that?" I swear, even as I said the words, I wanted to reach into the air and grab them, like fallen underwear, and pull them back on with a snap.

She looked at me a long time, until the light was green and she made a left onto the highway. When she spoke, her voice was fragile, sad. "I don't think anything is peachy dandy. I wanted to let you know who'll be there, because we are all greatly changed, including Terrence. The world's altered us as much as we've altered it."

I couldn't help imagining what had happened to Terrence, but it seemed maudlin to ask, and after my outburst, Phoebe didn't volunteer the details. How anything could seem more maudlin than this world we'd made for ourselves is beyond me, but propriety had always told me to avoid asking about afflictions, a remnant of my '50s training that actually stuck through the out-of-control '60s and onward. What a patchwork of eras I was, my own little history book with no definite point to it. Yet.

I remembered, though, my vision of a fiery beach, a few people in sand-adapted wheelchairs on the periphery. I wondered if one might be Terrence.

❀❀❀❀

We waited at the state park's gate for fifteen minutes while a ranger checked a few HOPT passengers and an Ecotram ahead of us for weapons and explosive devices. The bus was only about half full, but there were apparently lots of nooks and crannies to search, too many for one state agent to examine swiftly. Sitting in the stopped car after riding down the Coast Highway in silence was awkward. I knew better than I knew the aches of my elbows upon waking that I had behaved badly. "Sorry," I said. "You're right—I didn't care for Terrence. I just hate being called out on it." I shifted my bony old butt, ready to leave the car and walk around. I could already smell the damp ocean air.

"You're all right, Dess," Phoebe said. "We're old friends, in every important sense of the word." Then she began to hum the Simon and Garfunkel song of the same title—Phoebe and her nostalgic musical riffs, of course. They helped her through the days. I had no inkling what helped me though mine, except a desire to wake each morning, swipe the goop out of my eyes, and get on with what awaited me.

The bus finally pulled ahead and Phoebe stopped singing. The ranger beckoned us out of the car, patted us down, much to his youthful distaste, and searched our vehicle.

"Have a nice day, ladies," he said, tipping his hat. "Keep those hoods up on your robes. It's gonna be sizzling on the sand."

"Will do," Phoebe said, and saluted him. The ranger had no idea he was being mocked, which proved another advantage of old age: you could pull off what would have got you in trouble in your youth. Certain behaviors are, with time, forgiven as elderly kookiness instead of resented as the rudeness of upstarts. It's not all bad, being old.

She began to pull away, then braked abruptly. "Young man," she said, and waved him over to the car. "Say, can you advise us if there's a charging station for this old vehicle?" I couldn't see her face, and neither could he, but her voice sounded like she was batting her eyes behind the sun goggles.

"Might try Lot C. At the far end of it, used to be a plug. Probably is way overgrown now—you'll have to look for it. Good luck." He ducked into his kiosk and closed the door, finished with us.

"Thank you for your courteous assistance," she hollered, but he was out of earshot. She motored to Lot C, and I barely looked at the road for the expanse of shimmering water in front of us. "Do you see anything resembling an outlet?" she said.

I shook my head, squinting into the dead brush. I did see something that could have been a metal sign, a faded, unnatural kelly green color like all the state signs, when there had been money to produce them. It turned out, upon closer examination, to say, "Charging Station."

Phoebe scratched around in her pocketbook and produced a Swiss Army knife. "Here's the tool of the hour," she said, then pulled out a tissue and blew her nose. Women's purses never ceased being stocked with useful items, and nothing had yet been invented to rival a Kleenex for wiping away nasal drip. Simplicity still reigned in basic predicaments. The knife did not seem big enough for this job, however.

I said, "You have a machete attachment on that little thing?" It took several minutes of snipping, sawing, snapping and stomping creosote and sage to get to the plug-in, which crackled as Phoebe connected the car.

"That either means it's working or it isn't," she said, leaning away from the mini-shower of sparks. "If not, we can always spring for an Ecotram, or maybe hitch a ride with someone sympathetic to a couple of old crones."

"Speak for yourself," I said, and nudged her. She fell back on her butt, chortling. The sight of her there in the weeds made me laugh, too, and the magic thing about laughter is how many years it erases, the whole time you are laughing and for a short while thereafter. Everyone who laughs is young in that moment. Maybe the only reason to stay alive is for those small windows of glee when we forget ourselves—even the truly young live for them. God knows I misspent much of my youth trying to be older than I really was. What a waste.

"What's wrong with Terrence?" I asked when we stood to dust ourselves off and throw dirt over the hot sparks. "I didn't mean to sound like I wasn't interested."

"You'll know soon as you speak to him," she said. "He talks with a device. Bad case of PITS." Particulate Induced Throat Sarcoma was endemic to the dying world. Most victims of it stopped talking and the ones who had reason to continue went digital.

※ ※ ※

There are few days I regret you didn't survive, Theo, long enough to witness our sputtering planet. This was one of them. Suddenly, I remembered how breathtaking the ocean was, or at least had been, as it was on that fluke of a day. We pulled our loaded trolley along the path to the sand, chirping the way only old ladies and birds can do, with pleasure. The salt spray cleared our sinuses, and we helped each other bump the trolley down the steps, made years before of gravel and railroad ties. They now were more like suggestions of steps than steps themselves, but we managed them and spilled out onto the beach in our best underwear and FLOP—Final Level of Protection—robes. It seemed ridiculous to need protection from a day like this one, but we'd be in full sunlight for hours, that was true. It was also true that we were old ladies, riddled with wrinkles, liver spots, and skin cancers minor and major, and I was ashamed to be so cowed by the law of the land that had allowed the slow death of the ozone in the first place.

Catalina Island was visible, beyond the glistening water—a humpbacked silhouette in rusty smoke, for sure, but in view as it rarely had been for years. We gazed out at it, and several dolphins surfaced, close enough to shore we could hear their air intake. "What an incomparable day," Phoebe said, almost in a whisper. "I'm going to owe Bella for this one."

"You and me both," I said. And right then was when I thought of you, Theo, and how I would have loved for you to be with me to see the world as it once had been, as I had once known it. My eyes teared, and I had to use the sleeve of my robe to wipe them. If Phoebe noticed she didn't make an issue of it, but she did put her hand on my shoulder as we continued down the beach.

❀ ❀ ❀ ❀

"Helll-lllo, hel-lo, hel-lo," he said, using the cartoon voice of Loudmouth Lime, mascot for a powdered drink we guzzled as kids. Then, "Hello, schweetheart," in the voice of Humphrey Bogart, and then, "Hello, baaay-bee," à la the Big Bopper. Finally, Terrence Lambert used his own voice, digitally approximated, to greet us.

"Odessa Hauser, I presume?" he said, and bowed. He still had a full head of hair, white and bristly, poking out from his hood. "The years have been kind to you."

"Debatable," I said, and held my hand out for him to shake. He surprised me by kissing it. The custom was archaic when we were growing up—I wondered what that made it now. Prehistoric?

Phoebe, sun goggles atop her head, watched our exchange with amusement in her eyes, or maybe they were catching the shine of the sea. She leaned over and lowered his mask as she did her own, just for a second to kiss his cheek, as was the custom among close friends since face coverings became legislation.

"Let's arrange ourselves by the tide pools," she said, patting his mask back in place. "Eat some cheese, drink some wine. I've poured it in a Thermos. No one will be any the wiser, least of all the Lone Ranger up at his station."

"Kid's got more than his chip's capacity today," Terrence said and poked his index fingers into either side of his hood. "Systems overload."

We smoothed a wide, frayed quilt over the sand, where we sat, or maybe I should say, gradually lowered ourselves, making noises that we of advanced years mutter in sympathy of our joints. I remember swearing I'd never do that at one green time of my life when I glanced in the mirror and was able with makeup to amend the image that I saw. Now I simply accepted the image and turned away. Working with it took too much time, though not as much as it took to age me.

Phoebe instructed us to keep watch for Bella, but I wasn't sure how we'd know her from any other robed adult in the area. We were three of maybe a hundred others on the beach now, including the few children. I asked about the admission limit.

"Only a couple hundred," she said. "We left Bunker 321 just in time." She called all buildings *bunkers,* and that was our building's address, like the final count of a rocket launch.

"How'd you get here?" I said to Terrence, who was eyeing the goodies Phoebe pulled from an insulated bag.

"You mean, on the planet?" he asked, with his head cocked. He carefully took a dried pineapple ring, and slipped it on his thumb. "By the late-night sexual shenanigans of Doris and Bud Lambert."

"Tee hee," I said, and grabbed a ring for myself. "No. I mean here, the beach." When had I last used the expression *Tee hee*? The '60s? Terrence, the circus geek on stilts had grown into a man who spoke through a digital device, and he was making me behave like a twitch-butt of the first order.

"Hitched a ride on Ecotram." He twirled the pineapple around his thumb like a hula hoop. "Guess you can't call it hitching if you paid for it."

I grinned at him, but it was really at my remembered ability to flirt.

Honestly. The human body stores who we are like a locked cupboard of embarrassing pleasures.

FINAL LEVEL OF PROTECTION

How DOES IT FEEL TO swim in the Pacific Ocean after a decade of being banned from it, and after a half glass of wine in the hot sun? Like being engulfed by the hug of a long-missed grandparent. Like a poem of freedom or maybe surrender. Like a baptism where you feel the spiritual help immediately—my Lord, I came from this, and I am at home here.

I swam out beyond the wave break, and the water supported me like hands. It lifted me up. It also lifted the FLOP robe, which floated around me in a heavy island and made it extremely difficult to swim, and even more difficult to clamber out of the water. I told Phoebe as much when I splattered down on the sand beside her.

"I have an idea about that," Phoebe said, and her mouth moved slyly behind her mask, her eyebrows raising and lowering

À la Desi Arnaz, Terrence said, "Lucy, you have some splaining to do," but Isabella Pugliese arrived, and we fawned over her in gratitude for a good five minutes. A pair of binoculars around her neck, she brushed away our thank yous like kelp flies. "Why would I want to be here alone?" she said. "Of course I'm going to call my friends. Don't be ninnies." She was plump inside her FLOP robe, filling it out to capacity.

"Besides, I'm famished as usual, and who but Phoebe would provide the requisite delicacies?" The woman had a point; Phoebe had squirreled away a freezer and several cabinets full of food rarities.

Bella sat down on the blanket beside me, flesh jiggling as she settled, and Phoebe scrambled to lay out the rest of her feast of olives, crackers, a very hard cheese, and dried orange slices to go with the pineapple. I liked seeing someone who still had the gourmand's zeal for eating, even with the dwindling selection, someone who savored each bite, and I felt Bella's eyes on me when they left the food. "Looks like someone's already been in. You must be Dessa. Is the water divine?"

"Now that you mention it, yes, except the robe. I used to think one-pieces were too much coverage for water. This thing here is the Tent of Wrath." It was even heavier now that the wetness had crusted with sand.

"I told you, Dess, I have an idea." Terrence and I looked at Phoebe, and then each other, lifting our hands in common plea: Tell us.

Terrence even sang, "Talk to Me," in the voice of Sunny Ozuna, of the Sunliners.

"Don't sweat it, water babies," Bella said, licking a fingertip. "Phoebe's the queen of strategic moxie. She inherited the EV for next to nada, after all."

So we ate. Picnics were no picnic in these days of filter masks, where we'd lift them and lower them, bite by bite, sip by sip. Bella simply left hers cupped below her chin. "I like to enjoy my meals. As the observant among you may have noticed." After a while, Phoebe motioned us in the direction of the water, but only after some heated tongue-in-cheek about whether cramping really happens if you swim before digesting.

"What exactly does a swim-induced stomach cramp feel like?" Terrence said. "And how could it drown you, since it's only in your stomach?" His digital voice did sound remarkably like his own, except his words were compact when delivered, no fuzzy edges. I asked him how the device worked, and he explained it was similar to the Dot messaging device, except, instead of translating a voice into approximations of words, his voice chip translated thoughts to sounds. He had to be careful, though, to activate the chip only when he wanted to speak, otherwise people heard his random thoughts. He'd been embarrassed a couple of times when attractive women passed by. Of course, if he kept his mouth closed, the words were muffled, and he could look around innocently as though he had no idea who was talking.

"How in the hell can you find someone attractive in these hoods and robes?" I said to him.

"You know," he said softly. "You just know."

This made me wonder how the volume feature of a voice chip could read the tenderness of thoughts, but I didn't ask him about that.

❀ ❀ ❀

Phoebe's solution to the Tent of Wrath was a large net bag attached to a string, which in turn was attached to an old flatiron. An anchor sack. Bella stayed onshore, a happy sand Buddha as she continued feasting. The rest of us waded and dove beyond the breakers, while Phoebe informed us of her plan to disrobe and stuff the FLOP clothes into the sack.

"Are you sure that's a good idea?" I said. Going without sun-protection gear was punishable by hefty fine or worse. There was speculation that these laws were a throwback to our Puritan roots, another government excuse to keep us afraid and controlled. As an old woman, I'd kind of lost interest in such arguments, I'm embarrassed to say. It's impossible to spend an entire lifetime questioning authority. The friction of anything wears you down. You make concessions.

"It's an ingenious idea," Phoebe said, brightly. "Our robes won't float away from us. They'll stay in the sack exactly where we anchor them."

I firmly believed at this moment that all those years of studying happiness had imploded the logical part of her brain.

"I get the concept," I said, looking to Terrence for support. "I'm talking about the, uh, legal problem with it." Terrence stared out at Catalina and the horizon, avoiding the female fray.

"That's the fun part, Dess. And who's really going to give a radioactive rump roast about a bunch of old geezers in their underpants, submerged in water?" With that, she dunked beneath the surface, and pulled the FLOP gear over her head. Robe and hood gone, stuffed in the anchor bag, her poof of white hair looked to me like a beacon for the properly-clothed citizens on the beach.

Terrence finally decided to act as though he knew us. He checked out Phoebe, as much as anyone can check another person out when they tread in agitated water. He turned to me and said, "We are old, Dessa. If we can't do this now, when can we?" Reaching backward, he yanked the robe up his back, exposing his fuzzy gray shoulders and a bouquet of white chest hair.

What could I do? Two against one—I had to join my compadres. There was an unlegislated, timeless code about that, and anyway my skin chafed against the weight of the soggy robe. "Might as well," I said, and off came the Final Level of Protection.

We weren't naked, mind you. Just stripped down to a bare minimum.

❀ ❀ ❀ ❀

For the next hour, until the tips of our fingers and toes began to pucker like preserved fruit, we played in the water. Played. We tried to stay quiet, so as not to call attention to ourselves, but something about the sea and the waves—even small ones—made us delirious. The water performed its cool slide over us in our best underwear. Mine were scarlet boy shorts, and a big-girl bra built into a matching lace tank. I'd bought these for a special occasion I didn't believe for one second would arrive, and here it was. Underwear allowed for more individuality than the robes, and it usually remained unseen. Phoebe wore a modest ribbed cotton tank and panty set in her standard caramel, and Terrence appeared to be wearing plaid boxers, though the most apparent part of his swim out-fit was the bristle of hair on his head and the tufts of growth on his back, chest, and shoulders. That fuzz would protect him almost as much as his FLOP robe.

I rummaged around in the anchor bag for the baseball cap in my robe's pocket, and shoved it on my head. With bobby pins I always kept clipped on it, I attached the hat to what few curls I had to catch hold of. The bobby pin was an-other old-fashioned tool never improved upon. Some inven-tions simply survived, like we did.

With my hat in place, I let my feet drift up, and floated on my back, scooting around like an otter, trying not to stray far from my friends. This was territory I'd gotten away from, after all—both friendship and the ocean.

Then an urge blindsided me: I was seized by the desire to rub the hair on Terrence's shoulders. This brand of hair growth had never attracted me before. Quite the opposite. I sent one of my husbands to monthly appointments at a waxing salon, much to his manly chagrin. But all these years later, the sight of someone else's skin, especially a man's, was completely foreign to me, and the imperfections that used to make me cringe seemed charming. Enticing. Beckoning, even. Boney, sprouted shoulders. I don't know if it was a spell the ocean cast, or a spell of my own deprivation that made me swim up behind Terrence and put my hands on his shoulders, massaging them. "Fuzzy Wuzzy was a bear," I said, and tick-led him in his armpits.

"Hey," he hollered, swatting at me. "Hands off the mer-chandise."

I evaded him for few seconds, but the game was on. Phoe-be, Terrence, and I exhausted ourselves in a water-based tickle fight. There was much squealing and cackling, and if we'd meant to be the invisible old codgers we usually were, we sprang ourselves out of the mold that afternoon. Our bare arms and legs breached the water's surface. There wasn't a person on the beach who didn't know what we were up to. At one point, I remembered myself and gazed back at shore, where Bella was observing through her binoculars. Up on the

cliff behind her stood the park ranger in imitation of her attitude, watching us through his own special set of binos.

I waved to both of them. I didn't care who looked.

❀ ❀ ❀ ❀

As darkness approached, we had to prepare to leave the beach,
with no idea when or if we'd have such a day again. I'd not
had that kind of uncertain feeling before, back in the days I
left the shoreline believing it would be available indefinitely.
But dusk was the hour coastal hovercraft began patrolling,
and sent mobile officers in for arrests. We had already broken
the law once today. We knew it wouldn't be a great move to
break it again and flagrantly.

Phoebe, in her academic writings, devised a premise that
each person is at birth allowed a dozen extraordinary days,
some a few more, some a few less. We discussed her theory
as we trudged in our soggy robes up the path to the car, Bella bringing up the rear. We'd coerced her into the water, at
least enough to wade in thigh-deep where the waves broke
against her edifice of a body and cooled her down. She kept
her FLOP robe on. But even she proclaimed it was that kind
of a day for her. "What a frolic that was, boys and girls," were
her actual words.

I didn't say so, but if Phoebe's dozen were a real measure
of happiness, this was positively one of my allotments.

We exited the park, a full charge showing on Phoebe's
dashboard, leaving Isabella and Terrence at the Ecotram pickup across from the ranger's kiosk. The man in uniform eyed
us like teenvags as we left, and I made a point of stepping
out of the car and hugging Terrence Lambert about ten beats
longer than I should have. Terrence didn't seem to mind, and
said, "That was a pleasure from start to finish." He may have
meant the hug, the entire day, or both. Nobody cared about
precise meaning at that moment.

❀ ❀ ❀ ❀

Theo, you are not in my thoughts every moment like you used to be after you were born and soon after died, but you were with me again that day. It was the world I had hoped to bring you into, once I knew how much I wanted you, and the world I was glad you hadn't come to love only to watch it disappear. It glistened, it lifted, it soothed our fevered brows. On the way home, Phoebe chanted, "You li-ike Terrence, the guy you couldn't sta-and. You li-ike Terrence, and want to hold his ha-and." I called her an ancient bitch as I had when she got between me and the egg cartons. But if it weren't for that ancient bitch called Phoebe, a clear day at Crystal Cove wouldn't have found me in an ice age.

HEARTS, CRAZY EIGHTS, AND OLD MAID

TERRENCE BECAME A REGULAR AT Bunker 321, and instead of knocking he would call to us in the voice of a yodeler, or a movie gangster, or a Motown soul artist. We couldn't predict when he would pop by or the guise he would use when he stood at our door. He lived in a reclaimed dormitory, Sunset Village at UCLA, where he'd once taught History of American Filmmaking at the renowned school, a distinction that entitled him to senior adjusted-cost campus housing. Instead of students, dorms were filled with professors who'd outlived their usefulness. "I live in a mausoleum of knowledge," Terrence said. "Check me out, second vault from the emergency stairs." He joked about his arrangement, but the dorms had been adapted to be as comfortable as Phoebe's place, albeit smaller, which saved him money.

Getting from Westwood to the West Valley required that he take an Ecotram over the hill to the ancient, pot-holed Ventura Freeway. He disembarked at the corner of Ventura Boulevard and Topanga Canyon and walked a treacherous five blocks down the boulevard to the former insurance building that housed our floor. On his walk, he packed a water pistol filled with ammonia, in case he was accosted by teenvags.

He'd never had to use it, and carried nothing on him they could steal, but the squirt gun probably made him walk with more swagger than he might have without it. We fussed at him about the amount he must have been spending on these Ecotram sojourns, but he claimed our companionship was so beneficial to his health that he'd write the trips off as a medical expense. We were better and cheaper than acupressure and reflexology combined, and he would so testify to the IRS if anyone ever called him on it.

The IRS endured right along with bobby pins, Kleenex tissue, and us.

My dreams at that time were single-minded in nature, all of them involving—from Phoebe's song suggestion in the car, I'm sure—a warm, bristly-haired hand taking hold of mine. I wouldn't exactly say they were erotic dreams. Sometimes the hand felt gruff, and my own hand tensed and struggled at the confinement, but in other dreams there was a peaceful exhilaration in the way the hand left me feeling, as if I had been touched by the light of a star and a few stray flecks of it remained on me.

We usually didn't do anything special when Terrence came to visit. Phoebe and I had our fond routines of food preparation (toast being her favorite, brown rice with soy sauce mine), cleaning, wall monitor viewing, and board game playing. Old folks like us never quite took to virtual reality games the way young ones did. Reality was enough for us; we didn't want a clever substitute. Our favorite game was Rail Baron, where we imagined the thrill of cross-country train journeys, stretching our rail lines in tiny plastic cars over a miniaturized nation.

There were trips to the Superplex, during which Terrence would sometimes create a stir by singing an exact imitation of a rap song, and distract enough of the nimble crowd for Phoebe and me to move in and snatch up a prime item: a carton of fresh whole cow's milk, a plastic mesh bag of navel oranges, a shipment of Hershey's chocolate bars in the frozen foods section.

No matter how familiar a character Terrence became at

our bunker, I kept dreaming the dream of a hand holding mine, either by force or by choice, so the night he actually took my hand under the game table while Scrabble was underway, I did not twitch or start in shock. I entwined my fingers with his and kept them there until my turn to make a word. I calculated, in my head, that I hadn't held a man's hand for thirty-eight years. A long dry spell. My hand had that starlight feeling whenever he held it and the urge to have it again whenever we let go to place our letters on the board.

We did our best to hide our handholding beneath the table, but Phoebe eventually said, "If you want to bring your hands above ground, it's all right by me." Her dark eyes were full of merriment and collusion, even though the decision to hold hands had ultimately been Terrence's and mine.

Phoebe won the game with the word *zygote*. She cackled as she set the tiles in place.

Terrence stayed that night in my room, and lest I give the impression this meant we had gymnastic sex, I will say we most definitely did not. At first we just lay there on the bed, staring at the acoustic ceiling together, wondering why the government renovators hadn't changed out that feature when it had all other remnants of the former office building it had procured. We discussed what we'd naïvely thought our lives would be like in the future that was now, and discovered both of us had believed everyone, not just cops and bad guys, would own hovercraft vehicles and robots that served exotic foods from around the planet. Our only robot was an enormous wall screen that served us our personal and financial information as well as our daily entertainment. We held each other, and admitted being embarrassed by the skin tags, moles, barnacles, and other dermatological wonders that landscaped our once-smooth bodies. We apologized to each other for being so old, then laughed because we were both about the same age.

At one point, Terrence censored himself. He started to say, "I don't think I . . ." then stopped like a train once might have at a station.

We kissed, pulled up the sheets, and told stories about our

lives since high school. He had married twice and divorced, both times because the women were considerably younger and, as he said, "We became our ages." I said I guessed that wouldn't be a problem with us. We tickled each other's backs. At a moment we were kissing in earnest, Terrence said, "I'm afraid there's not much left of my erector set," and I replied it was fine because I couldn't have any more babies. I felt all right about that for the first time since my one and only brush with childbirth.

That's what Terrence had been thinking before, and almost let escape from his word-thought chip—that he couldn't have penetrative sex. But there are other affectionate and erotic acts to be performed and they're just as pleasant. Better than the supposed main event is the touch of someone's skin—hair, barnacles, and all—heated by the blood underneath it. Touch is how we begin our sexual lives and how we end them, with acts involving hands and mouths. Trusting another person to do what they will with your skin, to be next to it naked, is like opening a curtain to a window you've neglected to look out of, and suddenly there's a cosmic view. I didn't need Terrence to penetrate me. I needed him to touch me. We both needed to be touched, to exchange our mutual starlight.

Everyone needs to be touched, even if they think or say they don't.

When we had exhausted our old selves entirely, we curled up like hands at rest in a lap, and he began to stroke my hair.

"Nice to see you lose the baseball hat, Odessa," he said.

"Unh," I groaned, and put my face in the pillow. "Hair's so thin." He kept stroking my head, and it was neck-prickling comfort, despite my embarrassment over the patchy locks.

"It's just baby hair," he said, in a crooning way. "Baby fuzz. Little chick feathers."

The voice of one person speaking kindly can alleviate shame. I fell into a sumptuous sleep. From that evening on, the cap ceased to be part of my beauty routine.

❊ ❊ ❊ ❊

"You want Terrence to move in?" Phoebe dug at me with her

sharp, dark eyes, and I ripped the crusts from the toast she'd pushed onto my plate of smoke-dried turkey. Pushed without asking, I might add.

"Why would I tamper with a great arrangement?" I looked toward the wall monitor to avoid her gaze.

She paused and gave a sigh that had the annoying quality of being upbeat. How can a sigh be a happy thing, I wondered. Then I blurted, "You still haven't told me about your true love. The one you pine for in the heart of the night, and so on."

Phoebe regarded me as if my request to hear her story were a riddle or a trap. It wasn't. I wanted to know why she was devoutly unconcerned where it came to men. I stared right back at her. She knew all of my raw spots of pain and remorse, but I had an incomplete grasp of hers.

Another sigh, but this time it wasn't lighthearted. "He was a cowboy," she said, and I gasped. I couldn't help myself.

"Dess, you have to believe me. An honest-to-goodness cowboy. I couldn't make this up if I had cause to. He flew on a commercial jet for the very first time, and several times thereafter, to have trysts with me. He'd only been in a crop duster before that."

My mouth formed an O, then I breathed. "An academic in love with a dirt farmer?"

"Seized me with a force no theory could muster," she said. "But by the time I met him he was a cattle rancher, not a dirt farmer."

She'd been in Arizona in the early '90s, interviewing a revered Hopi shaman who also operated a tourist stop that sold fry bread and turquoise jewelry on the road to the Grand Canyon. He lectured about speaking her Truth and walking the path of Spirit, and how this led to happiness with a lower-case "h." Truth and Spirit were what eluded the white nation, which kept its people from their dreams. Happiness was not the point. Truth and Spirit were. She questioned the shaman, whose face was a wrinkled leather pouch, about why he ran the tourist trap. Was that the way of Truth and Spirit? He closed his eyes long enough to express mild irritation and said,

"It remains to be learned. I must live in all worlds, little seeker."
Phoebe was disappointed in the interviews; they yielded scant
material for her study. The shaman was slippery, difficult to
pin down as happiness itself. Over a period of two days, she'd
watched him turn showman when he worked the register, and
transform into mystic when he came back to her tape recorder. Her disappointment arose from her wish to admire the
shaman, but she'd found him human, not god or sage. She
concluded the interview like a petulant child rather than an
intellectual of some note in her field, hating herself for shar-
ing the guilt of his material weakness, which Americans of
every stripe claimed and denied by turns. Capitalism was the
disease we all caught.

What could she do? Exhausted, she took a room at a
Best Western with an acceptable Mexican restaurant and
bar attached, and went for a glass of unacceptable but much
needed wine.

That's when she encountered the cowboy whose name
was Gray Storm, another too-crazy-not-to-be-true detail of
the story. He sat at the bar, nursing a longneck beer, and said
to her from two stools down, "You look pretty much like
you had the same day I had, 'cept in a different setting." He
had tired green eyes that twinkled and large, strong hands,
and his day had started with one of his herding dogs being
shot dead by a neighboring rancher who caught the Border
Collie running off with a prize-winning lavender guinea fowl
in its mouth, and ended with his wife stomping out of the
house lugging a suitcase and their frightened eight-year-old
daughter, announcing she was leaving him and the godforsaken ranch and godforsaken vicinity forever. She wanted to
live near a city that had a department store where she could
buy herself a decent bra when she needed to.

Phoebe told him about her study and the shaman who
ran a tourist trap that made for a slight conflict of interests.
Gray just smiled. He had dimples, which further weakened
her good sense and resolve, and he did not say a disparaging
word about the Hopi or Navajo nations, as she expected he
would. He continued smiling and said, "Well, ma'am, you

chose a man-size project for yourself. Happiness and all. Yeah, I'll bet your quest has delivered more than a few gut punches." If anyone else had said something like that to her, she would have read it as chauvinism, but coming from Gray, it didn't feel insulting. It felt like camaraderie, and she liked the feeling, on that day and in that bar, of being a cowboy's confidant. Even though she wasn't sure what it meant.

That night, it meant he offered to walk her to her hotel room, and she accepted; then it meant the most astonishing sex of her life. Tender, heartbreaking sex; wild, sweat-breathless, romping sex; long, disbelieving stares at each other in between sessions. "Well, I never," Gray said during one of their breaks. Phoebe just shook her head, weakly. "I never either."

On the drive back to California, she was scathed. She felt as if she'd been dunked in water about to reach the boiling point and her skin was ready to fall off her bones. She figured that was that: scathed skin, unclothed bones, and she wouldn't see Gray Storm again, but oh my, what a night of incomparable sex to erase a troublesome day.

She was wrong, though. When she returned to her office at the college, there was a message on her machine. His daughter and wife had returned with a bag containing the new bra she'd wanted, and another bag full of apologetic work shirts for him, and ordinarily he'd be pleased about such a development, but he couldn't get Phoebe out of his mind. What were they going to do about that?

She made the long drive out to the Best Western several weekends in a row. Gray wandered away from the ranch as much as possible for quick assignations during the day, and for longer stretches in the evening or night. Phoebe didn't ask how he accomplished the absences.

"To be honest, Dess, I didn't consider his wife at first. The word *adultery* never tapped on my conscience. I thought toward when we would next be together. It was a fever that kept me from mulling over anything rational or ethical, a sickness, but instead of causing pain, the sickness took pain away. I was completely numb and stupid, except when we were doing the deed, of course, but I sensed on a cellular level, one I wouldn't let myself dispute, that the numb stupidity was a means that justified that end."

She was absolutely sure this was what people meant when they said they were madly in love: that they were numb and stupid, except when doing the deed, and then they were just stupid.

The affair went on in this way for nearly a year, Phoebe driving to him while he occasionally flew into LAX to her. He told his wife that he'd hired a fancy new tax attorney to economize at the ranch, and that arrangements were to be made for shipping cattle overseas from the port of Long Beach. When Phoebe doubted whether she'd buy the stories, he said, "My wife isn't into the finer points of Storm Ranch, so long as money's in the bank for spending. She's raising our girl to expect the same."

They might have continued their planned passion for quite some time if Gray hadn't asked Phoebe to move closer. The jet planes made him nervous and plugged his ears, often for a few days following his flight.

Phoebe, outraged, said, "And abandon my job? Just because your ears can't stand the pressure? You are joking, are you not?"

"I am not," Gray said, no give in his voice. An argument ensued about who would be most debilitated by the loss of his or her livelihood. Phoebe's job funded her research; Gray's job funded his considerable landholding and his family.

"So get a divorce," she said, but then he said he'd lose it all. He'd have to sell to settle with his wife who would, out of hurt, sue for more than her half.

It ended in a stalemate. Neither could forsake what they'd known and loved before they met, what was true to them and stable, the opposite of the frenetic pleasure they'd been chasing back and forth across the state line. She walked him to his gate at the airport, and said she hoped his ears would be all right after this trip home. He wished her luck with the happiness project. These were their final endearments.

"And on the strength of that recommendation for true love, you want me to bunk with Terrence?" I addressed her, though Phoebe's far-off gaze was over the long plains of a past I didn't share with her. "Hey, Phoebe, you call that love?"

She paused a little and pursed her lips into a grin. "I think of him after forty years. I smell his neck. I put my lips to it in dreams." She came back to the conversation, and said, "Are you in love with Terrence?"

Phoebe had once more begun to annoy me, but I was learning to keep myself patient by remembering how I used to be annoyed by people I didn't know, people who looked at me in a way I objected to, who bumped me on the sidewalk, or made a mess in a shared bathroom. I knew Phoebe. She was my friend. It made sense she would annoy me every now and then; it was the price everyone paid for friendship, and it was pretty reasonable.

"I love the time I spend with him. I won't volunteer more than that." I folded my arms in front of me with finality, and we sat for a moment until she started chuckling.

"Here we are, salty old broads who know less about love now than when we started out. Forgive me, Dess. I was momentarily seduced by the institute of happily ever after. I presumed it might work for you even though it never worked for me. Who knows why?"

"Amen, sister," I said. "Who the hell knows?" She gave me a sidelong hug, and we went off to our rooms to nap.

❀ ❀ ❀

That night after Terrence arrived, Phoebe said, "Let's celebrate," and bent down by degrees to her makeshift wine cellar beneath the sink.

"What for?" Terrence asked. He set a jar of jalapeno peppers on the counter, and tossed his squirt gun beside it.

"Because," Phoebe said, "we might as well." She uncorked a bottle of Sangiovese, and pulled a foil packet of freeze-dried avocado from the cabinet. "We'll sacrifice your jalapenos to guacamole."

Without being able to stop myself, I said, "Because everything's going to change, and one day we won't have all that we have here. It'll spill like a bowl of ambrosia." I looked over at Phoebe, who regarded me with a raised brow. Terrence didn't appear to notice the reference, savoring his first sip of wine and considering the plan for his peppers.

We dispatched him with two twenties to pick up some chips. Junk food was a heavily taxed luxury item; a bag of genetically modified corn tortilla strips cost around thirty-seven dollars, all told. He put his ammonia-filled weapon back into his robe pocket and trudged out the door, Roy Orbison serenading us with "Only the Lonely."

"Please explain," Phoebe said, brow still raised, "the cryptic outburst."

"It's true, isn't it?" I said, shrugging. "We're lucky to be here as we speak."

"Have you seen something? Something we all might need to know about?"

"Nothing specific." I never had a clear picture of what was to come, anyway, only intimations that made sense after the fact, not before. My gift was a few degrees more dependable than intuition. I just couldn't shake the dream of my hands being restrained, yet I understood the pleasure of Terrence holding them "We're fine for now, Phoebe."

Maybe in order to reassure herself, Phoebe rattled off a Greek myth involving ambrosia, the real stuff of the gods, not what we throw together as lowly humans. When the goddess Demeter wandered around Sicily and Greece in sorrow over the loss of her daughter to the underworld, she not only scorched the land, she posed as a beggar woman and punished all those who didn't offer her food and water. She turned a boy who scoffed at her rags into a lizard. One kind woman named Metaneira recognized Demeter as someone of regal bearing and gave her the refreshment she sought, also offering her a job as nursemaid for her infant son. Demeter hoped looking after the baby might ease the great emptiness she felt at losing Persephone. She cared for Metaneira's son as she would have her own. Each night, instead of putting him to bed in his cradle, she rubbed ambrosia all over his body, and placed him in the glowing coals of the fireplace in her room. Baffled by how quickly her son grew into an exceptional toddler, Metaneira spied on Demeter one night and, horrified at what she saw, burst into the room, demanding the baby be removed from the flames. Demeter changed back to her goddess form, and scolded the woman for preventing her son from becoming immortal, for her distrust of the gods. But, because Demeter had loved the boy, she promised he would have lasting honor if the family would build a temple in her name, which they hastened to do.

My heart clutched once when the baby boy was fed into the fire and again when he was taken from it, and though a small part of me wanted to make a flip remark about Phoebe's mythological interlude, a bigger part of me told the smaller part to be quiet.

Terrence crooned the same Orbison tune when he returned, "Dum dum dum dum dee do-wah," but the evening was anything but lonely. We played Crazy Eights and Hearts and Old Maid and went through two bottles of excellent, and very aged, red wine. We talked about the privilege of being old (sitting back and watching while everyone else felt compelled to jump in and screw things up even more than they already were). We bemoaned the loss of our favorite foods (green salads and shellfish). We remembered our favorite movie stars (John Cusack, his sister Joan, Fred Astaire, Katharine Hepburn, Vanessa Redgrave, Dustin Hoffman, Annette Bening, Anne Hathaway), all of them gone from movies and replaced by the young and tattooed, the pierced and the waxed hairless, and then the industry died out altogether when the rest of the economy heaved its final gasp. Studios recovered what they could when the government purchased rights to the films we watched on wall monitors with no prospect of anything new.

Post-buyout movies played in sticky theatres that reeked of unwashed and desperate patrons. Such was the updated history of American filmmaking, yet we felt wonderful in that room together, the rest of the world straining and withering outside. Call it escapism, but who are better entitled to it than the old with decades of memory pressing on them? We laughed, and did not feel, for that brief stretch of time, that we were dying.

On our swerving way to bed, Terrence took my hand, and Phoebe, behind us, warbled,

> And when I touch you I feel happy inside
> It's such a feeling that my love
> I can't hide, I can't hide, I can't hide

a song that for all the ages will be about the young of any social demographic.

Questions and Answers

Phoebe left at around eight that morning to avoid block-long lines at the Solarwear Outlet's two-old-for-one-new event, and Terrence ambled off to an appointment at the Medicarium. Medicare had been preserved like an endangered species by the Last Great Politicians, men and women who looked forward instead of sideways in fear. After the LGP, who were called socialists and worse by citizen droves while they were in office, we were essentially driven into a national sinkhole by what?

Question: Who ruined the country?

Answer: Who knew what to call them but ordinary men and women who quibbled over the meaning of patriotism, and the country they all loved crumbled around them as they talked semantics.

Terrence said, as he went out the door, "Time for a battery change."

About half an hour later, I thought he'd forgotten to Dot reserve an Ecotram stop, because he was back and hollering, "Open up. Federal agents." It wasn't the first time he'd announced himself in an alarming way. Then he pounded, hard.

After keying in the lock code, I swung the door open,

smiling, but within seconds found my hands tied by plastic restraints and my back flat against the entry wall. I stared at the identification cards of two serious men and a woman with narrowed, feral eyes.

"Why the . . . what . . . ?" and the female agent covered my mouth with a latex-gloved hand.

The man who had a green eye and a brown one shoved a photograph in my face. "Do you recognize these people?" he said, as if his power gave him physical pleasure.

I squinted at the photo. It was mostly turquoise ocean, with three bare-shouldered people swimming in it: Phoebe, Terrence, and me. "Yes. So?" I said.

"What were you doing there?" His badge said Agent Gamble.

"Swimming," I said, without hesitation. "Swimming on a Clear Beach Day."

"You have that right. It was an authorized day, according to our sources." Benevolence rolled off his tongue like rancid oil.

"Well, hallelujah for that," I said, and the woman clamped her gloved hand over my mouth again.

"You better keep that beak of yours polite," she hissed. "Bald-head, old one at that. We'll sew it shut if you can't control it."

I couldn't help being snide with this crew; they invited it. I said, "That would be interesting, since no one of your generation knows how to thread a needle."

She smacked my temple so hard with the heel of her hand the latex squealed on my skin. It knocked me out for a second, and I hit the floor, waking up seated against the wall. The three of them stared at me, hands on their weapons.

"Are we all happy now?" I said. I was dizzy, but considered it crucial not to show weakness. I focused on her face mask, how her breath blew the fabric in and out.

"We need to know whose idea it was," said the agent who had formerly been silent.

When I asked what idea, he said, "Being without Envirobes in a public place. A felony, in case you weren't aware."

I remembered the day well, remembered Phoebe convincing Terrence and me that no one would care if a trio of oldsters splashed around in our underwear. There was no chance I would betray my friend, though—not after the family she'd given me when I thought I'd go to the grave lacking closer association than the son of a wooly mammoth with whom I had a bathroom in common. Not after the rubber glove treatment old Slit Eyes had just given me. No. I couldn't turn my friends over to this crew.

"My idea," I spat. "From the start, if you really must know. If it's that important to you, which I hardly believe. Don't you kids have better things to do, like help people find shelter before they die of exposure?" I rubbed my temple, which was hot to the touch and throbbing through my tissue-papery skin.

"Every time someone breaks a law," she said, hand on her gun, "even bald grannies like you, all of society is put at risk." Her colleagues grunted in agreement.

I wasn't keen on being slugged again, so I remained silent, but thought about how ridiculous the term "at risk" was, applied to a people who'd dashed past that marker decades before without even slowing to notice.

The Silent One was becoming downright loquacious, his freckled cheeks pinking. "Ma'am, since you admitted, we're taking you in for a placement hearing. We can't wait here all day for your friends to return."

I said, "No need to. I coerced them, honestly. They were against it." I hung my head between my bent knees, and said, "I'm feeling like I might barf." Actually, I was dizzy but not nauseated. Mostly I was afraid of what could happen if Phoebe came singing into the house while our visitors were still here.

There was no reaction from my captors.

"You know hurl, upchuck, or belch to the ninth power?"

"We know retro-vernacular," said agent Gamble. "We're trained."

"Thank God," I said. "Know what a Ouiji board was?"

"Yes, we do," said Gamble while Slit Eyes gave him a viper's stare. I saw them in bed together, her eyes opened wide in violent pleasure. She was not his wife; if he had one, it was someone else. But he and the woman who'd decked me were lovers, guaranteed.

"Well, Ouiji board says I'm going to toss my breakfast on your shiny shoes if I can't use the bathroom in thirty seconds." I closed my mouth and choked a little, for realism's sake.

The three of them had a conference without words, and Slit Eyes—Agent Meckler, as her badge said—shouldered me gruffly down the hall. "Make it fast, bald granny."

I slammed the door and latched it, making vomit noises to rival a poisoned dog while Agent Meckler rattled the knob. "Unlock this, now!" she said in a voice deeper than normal, like a child giving a mock command. "You don't have locking clearance."

"How do I get that?" I said and gagged anew. I flushed the toilet, hacking and oh-gawding to cover up the noise of my search through drawers for a decent tube of lipstick. With a color called Smackaroo Sunset, I wrote on the underside of the toilet lid: *In Detention (naked swim). Send help.*

I closed the lid, and prayed that Phoebe returned home needing to pee. Women of our age most often did.

❋ ❋ ❋ ❋

I remained in Detention for six days, not even a week, but it was demoralizing enough that I convinced myself I'd be there till I died. I would have, if not for Phoebe and her connections.

Detention was nothing like what it used to mean when I was in school: sitting in an overly air-conditioned room under the supervision of a bored vice principal who flicked wax from his ears with a pencil tip. Detention now meant a football stadium converted into an open-air prison for mild-mannered criminals like me: people who stole food, lied on housing forms, or swam in a welcoming sea without Envirobes. Electric fences prevented escape from lower levels, and on upper level risers there was a laser field you'd be obliged to survive if you opted to take your chances and jump multiple stories to the ground. Chain-link fences separated the genders, and at night you heard the clang and rattle of male inmates scaling to find females. I did not worry. If any youngster of fifty climbed into my over-eighties enclosure looking for a good time, he'd be so delusional I could probably convince him his head was a cabbage on fire and to jump back over the fence to dunk it in a water bucket.

Heat was debilitating in the enclosure; tarp ceilings and occasional misting parboiled us like a Dutch oven of spare ribs, and the old skin itched and stung when I tossed around on my cot at night. My cell companions were either afflicted with dementia or behaved that way, pacing through their own worlds, talking to relatives and friends who were long gone or far removed, expressing a desire to die. "Why have I lived so long?" a tiny woman asked, whose body curled like an art deco question mark. One woman seemed lucid enough but hoarded garbage. She had built a wall of paper plates, cups, napkins, robe remnants, and dirt clods around what she viewed as her space in our shared area. She sat behind her creation, removing a plastic tray that doubled as a gate only when she had to use our putrid commode, which sat in the corner of our cell, shrouded by a sticky shower curtain. If I said something innocuous to her as she passed by, like hello, she replied appropriately but didn't pursue conversation beyond that.

While the violent were still kept in cinderblock penitentiaries that never released a penitent prisoner, we mild football field detainees were uniformly terrified, weakened, and sad.

I for one felt a little too sane, which didn't help me function in the madness. I heard every mournful howl and buzzing report of taser. I missed my friends at Bunker 321. I missed the saline smell of Terrence's fuzzy skin. I asked Corinne, the wall builder, what she she'd done, and she said, "My daughter turned me in for creating an attractive nuisance." She chuckled a bit after she said it, then surprised me with a rare elaboration. "I've always saved stuff. Used to be an artist." I pictured her standing, at some former time, beside a stunning wall of carved rock, welded metal, and molten glass. I saw her clearly and didn't doubt her truth.

"How about this gourmet spread?" she said, looking down

at her congealing plate. There were kidney beans floating in islands of grease, cardboard crackers, and a dollop of meat paste thrown on as garnish.

"Yum," I said. I was happy for dinner conversation, even with someone who seemed unhinged.

She made me think about the strange pattern of aging, how what makes for an identity at one point of our lives strips us of it later. A sculptor becomes a collector of junk, a caring teacher becomes an officious intruder, a wise politician becomes a cane-thumping tyrant or power-crazed pervert. We end up the quotient of the proud and dismal parts of our lifetime, plus remainders, and the remainders can be scary. The young reassure each other when they put us away that it's best for everyone, us included.

Question: Why are the young so afraid of the aged?

Answer: Because the young know they're next up and don't want to be reminded that all of us are headed down the same off ramp, no matter what forks in the road we choose. Every single one of us takes the last exit.

I was an ex-wife of rich guys I temporarily sold my soul to. I was the woman hoping to live long enough to buy it back.

❀ ❀ ❀ ❀

After dark, on the sixth day of my detention, a hand covered my mouth as I drooped from heat lethargy, and I thought I was done for.

Before I could protest, a raspy voice whispered in my ear. "Phoebe hired us. Don't be afraid." There were two of them, tall and dressed in black, and I had no idea how they'd entered the enclosure or how they'd exit, but I stayed silent. I knew I'd rather die in the act of freeing myself, even by way of some wrongheaded daredevil escapade—any circumstance but staying imprisoned in a slow-cook outdoor oven.

"Give me your left," the raspy whisper said, and I realized this was Pierce Dunn, Phoebe's younger brother who'd damaged his vocal chords in an adolescent suicide attempt. Here was another extraordinary man without a voice. "Drink this down fast. What we have to do here will hurt, but only for a moment."

I looked around the enclosure and saw my cellmates sleeping, all but Corinne whose eyes glowed and whose index finger came up to her mask in the sign of secrecy. Wild white hair sprang out from the nighttime release of her hood, and she looked like a deranged angel. I saluted her, which I meant as a sign of respect and gratitude.

Nola, Pierce's wife, handed me a flask of something reminiscent of gin mixed with chalk dust. It slammed my brain shut instantly and I watched the proceedings with removed fascination, as if the events were happening to someone else I knew very well. Nola grasped my hand in her two strong paws, and Pierce used a tool resembling an oversized hole-punch to stamp the Dot device out of the web of my hand. She sprinkled powder on the wound to stanch the bleeding, and wrapped the hand in treated gauze. That accomplished, she slipped Enviromitts over both my hands, "So no one notices while you're healing." Her calming whisper, compared to Pierce's rasp, was like spoken chocolate poured over my drugged mind. I trusted her smooth authority. Then I saw the canvas bag at their feet, and the body they bent to extract from it.

She was a woman my age and my size. Her hair was a similar rusted grey, like an ancient dog's stained muzzle. It was even thin like mine, or had been trimmed to look that way, and I honestly believed I was my own soul watching the body I was leaving. I wasn't frightened or sad at the prospect; I'd anticipated death for years and would have welcomed it, before I reconnected with Phoebe and began the new life at the end of my old and sorry one. The tongue hanging out of my corpse's mouth was a tad undignified, but for the most part I accepted my demise and thought maybe I had died from the Dot removal. Maybe the bytes of information on a chip and the GPS that tracked me were all that made me alive.

This theory fell apart as I witnessed Pierce stamping the Dot into the web of my dead body's left hand. I stared at my mitt-covered hands. I stared at the corpse's hand, which now bore my Dot device. My numbed mind couldn't make sense of these nighttime proceedings. Corinne stood and helped the couple slide my dead twin's body across the floor, lift her, and place her head on the pillow my head had been struggling to sleep on minutes before. Pierce and Nola murmured something to Corinne, who rummaged through her junk pile for a lacquered ceramic cross of the variety sold for decades by large-eyed kids at the Mexican border. One of those crosses lay on the chest of who I now was.

I remember Corinne kissing me on both sides of my face, then Nola and Pierce spiriting me off into the night of misters, group snoring, and slumped shapes of guards they'd drugged with gelatin darts coated in Memerase.

"They'll be up in an hour, guilt-ridden over their illegal naps," Nola said, her voice richly delighted. "That'll be all they recall, poor babies."

Pierce put his arm around her broad shoulders. "They'd be tasered with their own guns if they confessed," he said. "Detainees in your wing had a slightly higher dose, and a better than average night's sleep." By now we were outside the detention center, on the street, climbing into a deep purple hoverbug. I worried, even in my growing stupor, about flying in this contraption piloted by someone with a history of drinking.

"Phoebe said you're a drunk?" The statement came out as a question from my dry throat.

Pierce's laughter was like merry hiccupping. "You think she'd blab around town that her only brother was the Dot Robber? Being a drunk is my other identity. Like your dead Doppelganger back there in the cell."

As the tinny craft took off, I murmured, "Oh, I see," and lost consciousness.

❋ ❋ ❋ ❋

I came to in Bunker 321, with Phoebe and Terrence at my side, singing the *Cheers* theme:

> You wanna go where people know

People are all the same
You wanna go where everybody knows your name.

The voice chip continued to play the tinkling old-timey piano part at the end of the song, Terrence swaying with the notes broadcast from his musical mouth. Phoebe held my un-injured hand. "You need us now, dear Dessa. We're the ones who know you."

The Few Worldly Blessings

WHEN I AWOKE LATE THAT same morning in the bunker, Terrence and Phoebe were in my room, innocently asleep in the cushions of my rattan chairs. I stared at them while they slept, Phoebe at the foot of the bed and Terrence beside it. These were the people I'd taken the fall for, the people who saved me. Terrence kept his arms folded over his belly, as if he were digesting a big meal in his dreams. Phoebe's chin was on her chest and she snorted like a barn creature. The love I felt for them filled my eyes with tears. Friendship had made a pact with me in old age, and I was ambushed by it, powerless.

Much as I wanted to preserve the peace of that moment, I couldn't. A bolt of pain sizzled from my hand to my elbow, and I yelped. Phoebe stirred and resettled her chin, but Terrence threw his arms out from his midsection, stumbling to the hall, announcing, "She wakes, she wakes!" He returned with Pierce and Nola who'd camped out in Phoebe's room.

My feet twitched in reaction to the pain.

"Bad?" Pierce wheezed. He reached into his pocket.

"You did this to me," I said. "What do you think?"

Phoebe, now awake, said, "He rescued you, Dess," and just as I was about to make a glib, ungrateful remark—the pain talking, not my heart—Pierce jabbed a fleshy part of my hand beneath the thumb with a Darv-dart. The immediate relief silenced me, and I studied this intense, dark-eyed man, so sure in his movements, who had once been a gawky, troubled boy. In my life I've heard them called urchins, rebels, punks, juvenile delinquents, bikers, gang-bangers, skaters, angry young men, teenvags, you name it. But they're always just gawky, troubled boys, many of whom turn out to have a mission.

There are miracles, Theo. Even in a dying world, some of us grow to have courage. Some of us grow to have purpose. The double-lucky, like Pierce the Dot Robber, have both.

Nola dabbed ointment onto the wound and re-bandaged it, assuring me I'd be healed within a week. "But we'll have to move you before then."

I had scarcely appreciated my homecoming to the degree it deserved—the familiar smells of Phoebe's mildewed books strangely blended with the aromas of her stash of dried meats and vegetables, and the aura of safety that being with friends created. I didn't want to leave just yet. But even in a stupor, I knew that if Slit Eyes or anyone else from her Mod Squad had doubts about my death, here would be the place they'd come snooping. I looked up at Nola. "Move?"

"Of course," she said, her strong arm around me, squeezing and cajoling as if I'd forgotten something she'd told me before. "You're joining our team."

❀ ❀ ❀ ❀

If Pierce was the Dot Robber and Nola the Dot Robber's Wife, what did that make me? The Dot Robber Valet? Had I wished myself into my fondest fantasy? What, I wondered, could I possibly do for them?

One thing was . . . their shopping. Because they were tall enough to stand out in a crowd, and gaining legendary status as they spirited people like me away from unfair imprisonment, Pierce and Nola couldn't buy their own groceries. At five feet eight inches and shrinking, I was less conspicuous than they were, so long as I used different Magnabags, each trip a bag with a credit balance courtesy of a death at a Distress Center. There was no shortage of humble donations from the dead. Pierce and Nola kept at least three insiders at every nearby Distress Center to assist them in that regard. The desperate were always willing to take risks; it's the powerful who fight change, which makes change unlikely when promised by people in power. This was the riddle of our world.

I thought of crazy Corinne at the Detention Center and asked Nola how much of Corinne's story was true.

"All of it," she said, "except the crazy part. That's performance. Her daughter really had her detained for a purportedly dangerous collection of junk. Cory was so pissed she signed on to our cause." Nola examined the contents of the Magnabag I brought her, eyes glistening when she pulled out a package of genetically engineered dwarf carrots.

"Imported from Iceland," I said. I found them behind a stack of moldy, whitish, tomatoes. The sign said, "Perfect for Sauces!" If you were brave enough to lean over the decaying vegetable matter, you could find goods that store employees hoped to save for themselves.

As a team, Phoebe and I had sharpened our already superior shopping skills. I learned the best deals were no longer prominently displayed but secret or tucked away, like just about everything else worth living for: Clear Beach Days, renewable friendship, and freedom.

There was an evening of farewell with Terrence and Phoebe, and I often reflected on it when my new subversive self waited for a mission and deeply missed my old, recently rediscovered friends. Working with the Dot Robber duo allowed me to use the best of my talents, which were being prescient and being invisible, in that order. So many old folks think their invisibility is a curse, but it actually ranks up there with flight as a superpower. All an elderly invisible needs is a dose of purpose, and she can work small miracles. We are the ones who have the wisdom to do so. The young don't remember a world before hope became a liability instead of a gift. We knew that world. Our hope hung on the way fruit sometimes clings to dying trees.

The farewell bash was spur-of-the-moment; Nola and Pierce thought it best for me to steal away with them to their Topanga lair post haste, so Phoebe threw together one of her signature feasts of heat resistant noshes and bent under the sink for successive bottles of wine. I watched Pierce, since he was the Hoverbug pilot; he drank nothing but water filtered from a government-issue pitcher we were given each time we exchanged our robes. Nola indulged, though, and laughed a kind of liquid laugh whenever Terrence turned on his musicality, crooning Drifters, belting Maria Callas, twanging Hank Williams. He was delighted to be delighting someone, and the rest of us were delighted to watch him at it. I was downcast at the thought of being without his nightly visits and kisses and starlight closeness.

That's the wonderful thing about friendship, Theo, another one of the few worldly blessings I'm sorry you missed. When you're without friends, thoughts and feelings wind around inside of you like tumors formed of knotted hair. When your friends are with you, the lonely thoughts and feelings have a tendency to untangle, to either make more sense or make no sense at all and be dispensed with. We humans aren't meant to be alone. Our purpose is to reach for each other. But the world grew into a place where machines, bureaucrats, and their sloganeering minions did the reaching for us and we lost our way.

Here's something hilarious: the government became so dependent on Dot technology, on keeping track of people by chip implants, that their removal made bodies anonymous. Detective work—tracing fingerprints, footprints, DNA—became extinct as a profession, along with teaching. There were those among us who took advantage of the loss and freed ourselves by losing our identities.

If the authorities wanted to find me, they would have to do it by sighting, but I was certifiably dead, and my Dot in a dead hand would be all they needed to convince them of that falsehood.

Terrence kissed me goodbye like someone who knew me well, and Phoebe hugged me the same, and it felt so right to be known by the good people and out of range of the bad that I almost enjoyed the dull pain that had placed my vital statistics into a cadaver. I told them my tears were from my hand, but they laughed because they knew better.

❈ ❈ ❈

We arrived at the Topanga lair when it was dark; Nola and I were merrily, leglessly drunk. Pierce shushed us with a fatherly scowl and head shake, motioning for us to help clear away an arrangement of brush and Manzanita that disguised the cave's entrance. Fifteen feet inside the cave was a double door that opened to a dwelling, not the least bit cave-like.

No condensed water dripped from the ceiling, no bats swooped our heads, and no moss grew on the walls. It was a plastered, whitewashed greatroom, dry as the matted dust coating the teak furniture. "I don't do cave cleaning," Nola said, and tapped my ribs with her elbow. "I have bigger jobs on my agenda." She rolled her large eyes toward Pierce.

I suppose the painkiller and alcohol made me easily entertained, and because I was relieved that I was out of Detention, I began laughing like I had in my dream of Phoebe with the flower sticking out the top of her head. "Yeah," I guffawed. "You certainly do." I could not stop laughing, and Nola joined me, chortling herself into my hysteria. Not even Pierce's scowl could quiet us until the flurry of laughter played itself out.

Laughter and tears, Theo, can take on a life of their own, like the viruses and cancers that destroy us. Laughter and tears are our best defense for being human.

As I got my breath back, I looked at Pierce, now smiling from having no choice but to witness his wife and me, and he said, "The guy who built this place was a survivalist, and guess what? He died."

Pierce laughed in hiccups, a burst of rapid-fire squeaks that started Nola and me going again. It was close to ten minutes before we were sore enough in our cores to stop, and we spent some additional moments gearing down, wiping our eyes, sniffing, and having involuntary syllables of dying-out hilarity. Then we were silent for quite some time, staring at our hands, the bright white walls, the tiled floor. Finally I said, "What are we revving up to do, pray tell?" I had a hunch that breaking and entering Detention centers wasn't the apex of Pierce's plans.

"Make the revolution that never happened," Pierce said in a rasp between shallow coughs.

"We might as well," I said, and then I wondered, How? until I curled up on the couch cushions and crashed out.

Tiebreaker

And so I lost my Dot, my identity, and became what I always wanted to be: an outlaw.

At first, I was only a sidekick who bought groceries for the main outlaws, but gradually I joined in on their big ventures.

I didn't know the nature of any mission until we were airborne in the Hoverbug, which was nerve-wracking in itself. Pierce navigated by sight, and our forays usually happened at night, so we wore night-vision goggles and kept our eyes trained for obstacles: another vessel at three o'clock; a remnant telephone wire, dead ahead; a flagpole at eleven o'clock. A primitive system, but we couldn't risk using actual radar and alerting others to our presence. Mainly, we were concerned with police craft, and when we saw the chartreuse glow strips that identified them, we dropped quickly to the ground or a nearby flat rooftops, and stayed till it was clear.

Sometimes we picked up bodies at Distress Centers and delivered them to a woman called the Shape Shifter. She lived in a cabin overgrown with vines and witchgrass, and Shapey, which was her nickname, altered the bodies for identity-switch missions. Mostly, she worked with hair and skin color, even eye color, and tried to make a decent match, adding a skin tint and mole here, a birthmark or tattoo there if it was part of a government description. Shapey's most critical job was removing the corpse's original Dot and forming a flesh-colored and -textured plastic casing into which the new Dot, taken from the rescued prisoner, would snap. Both Nola and Pierce marveled at her flawless work. Shapey, whose real name was Alexandria, had once been employed by Paramount as a make-up artist. After she lost a dear friend to the heat and neglect of a Detention Center, Shapey came up with the body-swap idea, discussing it with Nola, her neighbor.

Small plans can turn into larger ones.

As the grateful rescued began to ask what they could do to help the cause, Pierce told them to keep the secret and wait for further instruction. A corps developed.

We continued delivering bodies to Shapey, picking them up prepared, and enacting the exchanges at Detention Centers. I made the job of carrying dead weight much easier for Nola and Pierce. Tall and tough as they were, they had a long way to bend and lift; a third set of aged muscles was a relief to theirs.

They never trained me in the use of the Memerase darts. Nola asked me once if I wanted a gun of my own, but I declined. I said, "I'd probably shoot myself with it, and not remember what the hell I was doing here with you."

"You have a point," Nola said, and we giggled at her pun.

I now had two more friends in the bargain. They were not quite as much fun as Terrence and Phoebe—Nola and Pierce had to be discreet, after all, and they had much on their minds—but once in a while, after a frantic, fast-paced body exchange, the newly-sprung prisoner delivered to the apartment of a supporter, we would celebrate our good work with a meal of hard cheeses, nuts, and wine. Pierce never imbibed. When I asked him whether drinking had once been a problem for him, he said, "Once, and several times over." He glanced sheepishly at Nola. "I might put myself through it again, but not Nola." She regarded him with the complete grasp of who he was. It is not easy to know a person that well, but such knowledge is the nourishment of love.

"Damn straight," she said, and looped her arm around him.

I did not know you that well, Theo, but I hope through all this you will come to know me.

❀ ❀ ❀

My favorite responsibility hinged on evaluating people who needed our help. Pierce and Nola took a full profile of the detainee from the requesting party. They asked about the jobs a person held, his or her criminal record, and history of police or government work. Not all government workers were taboo, but if the job had anything to do with investigation, detention, or intelligence, the candidate was denied. All police work and any history of violence typically led to instant refusal.

Most of the time, Nola and Pierce agreed on the eligibility of a candidate, but they summoned me as a tiebreaker. Strangely enough, most tiebreaker situations involved violent crime and extenuating circumstances, rather than police or government work. One woman had killed an abusive husband, served ten years in a penitentiary, then was thrust into a community much changed and a dwelling much like the one I feared I'd live out my days in, with a shared bathroom. This woman ended up in a Detention Center because she attacked the bath sharer, whipping him with a soggy towel he'd left mildewing on the floor for over a week. The bath mate said she'd tried to strangle him with the fetid towel.

I don't have to say which way I broke that tie.

Not all of the decisions were so easy. One candidate was a teenvag in Detention for knocking down and robbing an old woman—much younger than my cohorts and me, might I add. This woman was in her early seventies. She'd shattered a wrist and an elbow in the fall, but forgave the boy because he Dot messaged her at the Medicarium to check on her recovery and sent a Detention Center courier with a Magnabag to replace the food he'd stolen. The seventy year-old, in fact, was his petitioner for being freed. She signed an affidavit that claimed she "trusted him like her own family." Poor thing had no family left, like so many of us. I sat with this case for a day or two, because, well, maybe the boy had just been desperately hungry. Maybe he truly regretted what he'd done. But something didn't seem kosher about the case, and I had a recurring vision of the teenvag twisting the broken elbow behind the woman's back, and her wincing in pain. I encouraged Nola to have someone at the hospital—an ally of theirs—sit down and talk with the victim, and sure enough, she eventually produced a note hastily stuck to the back of his apology card in the Magnabag: *U dnt stnd up fr me, my frnds outsde wll find u & pt yr ass awy fr good.*

When the Medicarium released her, Shapey worked her magic on the old woman I hesitate to call old, and we relocated her for safety's sake in a room with a supporter in a distant Northern California neighborhood.

One of our most ardent supporters, a guy we called Cellman, was initially a tiebreaker situation. His violent history started at a movie theatre, back when there were legitimate ones. Someone down the row from him was texting, since there were still cell phones, and every time a new text arrived a goat bleat announced it. Cellman politely asked the texter to stop but was ignored. The texting and bleating went on for another fifteen or twenty minutes, at which point Cellman got out of his seat as if he were going to the restroom, snatched up the offending cell phone, and ran it out to the lobby, where he crushed it under his heel, then threw the useless apparatus out the front door into the path of an Ecotram dropping privileged youngsters off for a late matinee.

The fist-fight that followed landed both Cellman and the texter in jail. For a few days, only.

Then, in his late fifties, Cellman was in Detention for stabbing a man, a government worker, who served him with an eviction notice two days after his wife died from a virulent particulate cancer. "You are no longer eligible for married housing, sir," the worker announced. "You'll have to move out in two weeks' time. It's the maximum allowed for bereavement."

Cellman excused himself, claiming he'd left beans cooking on the stove. He held the knife behind his back, returned, and deftly stabbed the worker through his left hand so that it was impaled on the tablet it hovered over, urging Cellman to sign. "That's not for the eviction notice," Cellman said, putting his signature on the bloodied screen, "but for taking my wife's body and burning it before I had a chance to say a proper goodbye, you efficient sons of bitches." Bodies were, by edict, whisked off to the crematorium as soon as a death certificate was issued: with so many bodies to process, there had to be a uniform system in deference to public health, so we were told, and families had no say in the matter.

Cellman was in Detention for life; he avoided the penitentiary by virtue of his age. Anyone approaching sixty was no match for the weight-lifting gladiators of the pen. His advocate was Isabella Pugliese.

"I worked with this man," she warbled. "He's a pussycat, brilliant PR person for Friends of the Earth back in the day. He could be of great assistance to your cause, angry about all the things you hate, loathe, and despise—whatever's the hold-up?"

I wondered what in the world the cause was, besides rescuing people from Detention, and became increasingly miffed because I was playing along in a game whose outcome eluded me.

But, upon seeing Cellman's photo, I argued in his favor. I recognized him—a certain curve in his posture and flatness at the back of his head—not from any real occasion, but from my vision of the beach, with palm trees illuminated orange along with Phoebe's hair. Cellman walked across the screen of that tableau; I had seen him there, and though I didn't know what that scene meant, I knew that there was power in it.

Although Nola brusquely countered, "He ran a guy's hand through with a carving knife, for God's sake," I broke the tie. I rescued Cellman.

I did not mention my beach vision. I admitted I'd been tempted, several times over, to crush cell phones, especially when I heard people conducting extremely sensitive conversations in public—like breaking up with a spouse or lover, or discussing a medical problem, such as a bleeding ulcer or genital warts. Who wanted to hear that much personal data about a stranger? It was like having your nose rubbed in a reality show you couldn't switch off. Yet for a long, long time, we inflicted such unwanted intimacies on each other, and only whispered about the neglect of the old and the poor, and the favor shown the spectacularly rich, and the burden of responsibility that ruined the middle class, all of which we should have bellowed about into our cell phones, all problems that collapsed the way of life we'd come to expect forever.

I also admitted to Pierce and Nola that I might be capable of stabbing a person who denied me the right to bury someone I loved the way I saw fit. I didn't mention you, Theo. Only Phoebe and Terrence knew that story.

Thus, we rescued a man to help our cause, whatever it was, a PR person who would have to do undercover PR, a slightly perplexing job description.

One slow night at the cave house, as Pierce snored in their curtained room—"A wink at privacy, all we need at our age," Nola had said—I asked her the question: Aside from rescuing detainees, what, exactly, was the cause, and was there a plan in place that I didn't know about?

"It's taking shape," Nola said, a sharp eye toward the curtain. "Listen, I hate to seem like I'm hiding anything from you, but I want Pierce to be in on this discussion, too."

"Is this a facts of life lecture? What's the big secret?" I tried not to let my indignation show, but, honestly, did they expect me not to wonder what was afoot? They rescued me, but that didn't make me an indentured servant.

Nola looked at me with concern, as if I might suddenly pull out the hand-stabbing knife. "You are a godsend, Dessa. You've made our lives fuller and easier. But this is a matter we need to discuss dispassionately. Have a cup of mint tea and calm down—I'll wake Pierce."

Dispassionately. That was a Nola word, all right. I made some tea and tried to settle my heartbeat. I didn't want to keel over dead before I performed my crowning achievement.

❊ ❊ ❊ ❊

We were staging an insurrection, Pierce informed me. The details of the time and place were not finalized, nor were the logistical concerns of how people would get there, how the protest would be conducted, how people would leave, how they would later be resettled. But it was in the making. It would happen.

"Could you be a little more specific?" I said. "I might be risking my life for this extravaganza, and I think I'd like more in the way of nuts and bolts."

Nola sat on the couch, watching, her hands dispassionately folded in her lap. My hands were on my hips.

Pierce understood my concerns. He really did. He wanted to assure me that he would not submit me to any danger that he was not willing to face himself. That Nola was not willing to face. If I wanted out of the arrangement, they had other supporters who would take me in, and I would be free of the risks they were about to undertake. It was entirely up to me. Unfortunately, for my anonymity's sake and for the sake of Phoebe, and Terrence, who'd moved into my room since my imprisonment because Phoebe was anxious alone, I wouldn't be able to sidle back into that old arrangement.

Well, fine, now I was being kicked out of the cave house for requesting information I still did not know. That didn't seem fair.

He replied in the transformed voice of a man who had lisped my name as a child. "You are like family, Dessa. All right, I'll tell you as much as we know at the moment, but you must not worry about it. We haven't told you because we want it to be like our other missions—we just go and do the thing and get it done well with a modicum of fuss. Here's what the event will be: a mass Dot destruction."

I must have stared at him for a long moment, absorbing this information. "You can't be serious," I said. "You couldn't have enough of those hole-puncher thingies to do that on a massive scale, and besides, the medical problems that might occur would be huge. Think of the infections if they're not properly treated."

He assured me they had thought of that. Nola stayed put, hands folded in her lap, a beatific smile on her face.

"Do you remember that game we used to play as kids, What If?" she said. "Maybe it would help if we played that now. I'll start. What if we found a method more effective and less dangerous than the current hole-puncher?"

I said even so, you couldn't do it on a large scale. My hands, I realized, were stuck on my hips and I dropped them to my sides where they had trouble holding still.

"What if we had the volunteer force that says we could?" Nola's posture shifted a bit on the couch, but her hands stayed in her lap. Her head tilted at me.

"How would all those people—there would have to be droves of them—keep a secret?" I needed to sit. My mouth was dry and I was lightheaded. I plopped down next to Nola on the couch. "Where would they go to live?" I said. "Where would they hide when the authorities came looking?"

"What if they kept a secret one person at a time, just like we do? What if there were cells of us in place all over the state and nation?" Nola looped her strong arm around me in her inimitable way. It was a difficult force to resist. Not even Pierce could.

He said, "What if we've had people refurbishing interiors of abandoned homes? You know, all the homes that no one could pay mortgages on, then the banks repossessed, then all the banks became one bank that didn't care about home loans anymore? You know, those houses? All over deserted communities, all over the country?"

"You have that many people working for you?" I said.

She said, "Yup, the movement does, remaking homes to be off the grid, like ours."

He said to me, "What do you think is the worst that can happen?"

"We will all be captured and thrown in Detention."

"You think they have the means to capture and detain that many people in one fell swoop?" Nola asked.

I guessed they'd just pack us in like grains of sand—they wouldn't care if we starved or suffocated.

Pierce said that by sheer dint of numbers we could easily force an escape.

"What if they don't bother to capture us but shoot and kill us all from the air, like bounty?" I had always been proficient at foreseeing doom.

"And?" Pierce waited for my reply.

"And, I won't get to see Terrence or Phoebe again." My voice shook and I began to cry. I used to avoid crying in front of people. What was happening to me? Friendship had softened me like an old shoe, and I could comfortably walk straight through where I would have taken a detour before.

"What if we tell you that you will see Phoebe and Terrence, and they will be there participating? Would that make it easier on you, no matter what transpires?" Pierce grinned at me, the strange, sensitive little boy in his smile.

He had a point. If I could see my friends—if I were with my friends—I would be willing to see the insurrection through and die. Our time was about to come sooner rather than later anyway.

❀ ❀ ❀

What followed was an extremely busy time for us, only we weren't doing what we used to do, transferring bodies and identities. We embarked on visits. I don't use the word as code or euphemism. We actually visited former prisoners whom Pierce and Nola (and in some cases I) had freed from Detention centers. These visits were grass roots work: we wanted to see how the rescued were faring in their new locations and let them know what was coming next. We couldn't Dot message this mission or broadcast it on wall monitors, especially since many of us were without Dot devices. I was reminded of this each day when I felt the small, healed opening in my left hand, not unlike the gradually stretched earlobe holes fashionable among youth of a certain era.

Ours was an underground society, part of a family of Dot Robbers active in cities all over the country: New York, Chicago, Philadelphia, Atlanta, Seattle, St. Louis, Oklahoma City, you name them, all but Washington DC. That would be too risky. Too much intelligence mayhem there. Why people still called it intelligence I did not know. What we were doing seemed much more intelligent.

We targeted specific buildings of our area, greater LA, and asked the folks we visited to contact friends and supporters they knew by having a small gathering: a night of bridge, a wall monitor movie fest, a simple dinner party. They needed to have an ostensible reason for the gathering other than "the plan," and the members of the gathering had to be eminently trustworthy. People who'd lost loved ones in Detention or Distress Centers, people displaced, angry, and dissatisfied with their sequestered lives. People who were willing to take risks to live the life they wanted, instead of dying afraid and cowed.

Were there many of them? Amazingly, there were. I was skeptical at first; I knew if I hadn't run into Phoebe that day in the Superplex, I would still be counting off my sorry days with Son of Wooly Mammoth. I thanked every star alive or dead in the heavens that brought me to that egg display at that time, in that place, and gave me life at the end of my days.

As it happened, there were others at various stages of their lives, looking for just such a purposeful chance.

There was the émigré from what was once Yugoslavia, who as a young woman, filled with the dreams America offered her, opened a small bookstore in Pasadena and made it a success. As grey streaks appeared in her hair, the government banned book sales, except on wall monitors, and she chained herself to the shop's antique cash register. That's what landed her in Detention. No one had to invent her nickname—it was Punkiedoodle, her term of affection for all regular customers. "Hallo, Punkiedoodle," she would say, and it's what she hollered when she realized Pierce and Nola were paying her a visit. She actually used a plural of the endearment.

Punkiedoodle assured us she had many, many friends who would be happy to join the cause. She would have to have five or six parties for them.

Then there was Doctor Shaft, former Ecotram and Hoverbug mechanic who lived in a 1960s bomb shelter in the hills of Laurel Canyon. He'd been incarcerated for supposedly causing a police craft to crash. "Mechanical failure due to maintenance error," was what the report called it, when anyone at the scene smelled the fumes of alcohol still rising from the pilot officer's boneless body.

Shaft, one of Pierce and Nola's first rescues, was every bit as imposing as Richard Roundtree and would help us secure transportation to and from the event. His colleagues, down to the last of them, knew he had taken punishment that could just as well have been leveled upon them. They were relieved to assist.

The only rescued people not willing to use their contacts or skills to recruit were those too ill or infirm to take a lengthy ride, much less that kind of risk, who needed all their energy to breathe their finite breaths.

To my astonishment, and according to estimates coming in from contacts, there were hundreds, maybe thousands, planning to attend the event. Pierce, Nola, and I sorted through the handwritten notes delivered to a strongbox inside a hollow oak near our place. Cellman oversaw the deliveries, using a troop of his supporters, surreptitious and brilliant. We neither heard nor saw a trace of them.

We kept the solar lights dim, the cave somewhat stuffy, but were giddy as expectant parents who'd just seen the toes and fingers of their developing child in a sonogram. The plan was doing more than taking shape. It was coming to life.

❀ ❀ ❀ ❀

Out of the goodness of their hearts, or perhaps out of fear that I'd melt into tears again, Nola and Pierce juggled one of our visitation outings so that we'd spend the night at Phoebe's. Seeing Terrence and Phoebe after an absence of a few months was like rain, a blessing that rarely happened anymore. I felt lightened and clean.

"You're a genu-wine hero," Terrence techno-whispered in my ear, as he leaned in to kiss me.

"I'm a heroic assistant," I said. I was reminded how familiar and foreign a kiss could seem, all at the same time, if you'd been without one for a while. A shock, albeit pleasant, that forced the brain to recalibrate.

Phoebe was hugs and tears and kisses all around. "So much to catch up on!" she said. Her hair had grown out longer and the weight of it made it straighter, not quite so poofy. She whipped out the freeze-dried avocado and some curried hummus mix, and located a jumbo bag of our favorite genetically manipulated corn tortilla chips, which she asked me to put in a bowl for her. Of course, she bent down to her wine cellar under the sink. There was always her wine.

"Honestly, Phoebe," I said, "What is the source of all this vino? It seems endless."

"I was frugal and careful—you remember how I was, measuring my words and deeds. Now it's paying off. Most people our age don't have the benefit of so many loved ones, and I don't have to be a sad old acquisitive woman, dying with her wine collection intact. Drink it up."

Phoebe was revved and brought out a Yahtzee game, the cardboard box flapping at corners, the dice without paint. We'd have to count indentations.

As I bore the tortilla chips to the coffee table, Terrence startled me, blowing on my neck and kissing it from behind, and the ticklish shiver this induced made me lose my grip on the ceramic bowl, which fell to the bamboo floor and shattered, chips and shards mixing it up.

"OOPSIE-DAISY," Terrence said in the voice of a slapstick comedian I didn't want to recognize, probably Jerry Lewis.

I wasn't amused at all. In my current anxious, emotional state, I thought the breakage tragic. I looked at Terrence, my beloved, with fury in my eye, and then felt guilty for doing so. I started to sob, crouching to collect the pieces.

Phoebe was immediately at my side. "Dess, honey, it's only a bowl of chips. It's not an omen—you have to trust me on that. I have another bag in the cupboard. The bowl is just an ancient, cheap tchotchke from Mainly Seconds. Most likely contains lead."

Terrence and Pierce gently lifted me up and sat me on the couch. They placed a box of tissues and a glass of wine in front of me. "Choose your poison, little lady," Terrence said, John Wayne style.

I grabbed a tissue, honked my nose, and through my sobs carried on about what a clumsy idiot I was, and how I didn't deserve to be in the company of such good, gracious people who clearly had more going for them than I could ever hope to, on and on, the poison of self-doubt pouring out of me like bile, foul and draining. When I finally had expended myself and regained the presence of mind to make eye contact with the people clustered around me, I knew they would bear the look of disgust to which they were entitled, but instead, I saw them grinning.

"What, you think this is funny?" I grabbed the wine glass and took a slug.

Pierce was first to speak. "Um, yeah, kind of. We've all made crazy missteps like that, Dessa. But we learned from them and that's why we're here, including you. And we're trying to forgive ourselves, more or less, in the same uneven way you are."

"You're not unique," Terrence said, touching my face. "We're a garden variety of schmucks and schmendricks."

I silently finished my wine, staring down at the coffee table while Phoebe sang,

> Don't let it bring you down
> It's only castles burning
> Find someone who's turning
> And you will come around

Nola poured me another glass, and the Yahtzee game ensued, amid Pierce's hushed description of the developing plan: Shapey was working with a medical engineer to create a removal kit that punched out the core of the Dot, but left the rim in place, eliminating the risk of cutting skin. Then the kit had another piece that would punch in a fitted piece of silvery plastic that resembled a Dot at first glance. Punkiedoodle and friends arranged teams to hand out antibiotic packets to any whose aim was not true in the punch-out process, and there would be a volunteer medical corps of retired doctors and nurses if stitches or other intervention seemed necessary. Cellman kept count of pledged participants and facilitated delivery of the count to our mail drop. He also kept Doc Shaft current with the pledges so that adequate transportation would be available. The good Doc was really having to scramble as the count grew.

Terrence said, "You employ the Seven Dwarves."

Pierce responded, yes, it was a secret society working for a common goal, except that there were other sects around the country, waiting to see how our event went, in order to implement their own. As California goes, so goes the nation, Pierce said, or at least, we would be testing the truth of that maxim.

I listened, rolled the dice, and used my old Yahtzee strategy of filling in every blank possible before giving up on the five of a kind the game was named after. It was like going for broke. I wasn't about to let an old superstition about anticipation and loss keep me from doing possibly the most important thing I'd ever been asked to do. When I rolled my first Yahtzee, I jumped off the couch as fast as any octogenarian can jump, and creakily twirled around with my hands in the air. But, when I rolled my second Yahtzee—in ones, no less—I stayed put and gloated.

"We just let you win because we felt sorry for you," Nola said, deadpan.

"You know what I'll miss about this Dot device?" Phoebe said, fingering hers with something like affection. "I'll miss how the messages float up out of nowhere, like fortunes on those eight ball toys we had as kids. Remember those?"

We all nodded that we did. Then Terrence said, "Chances are good."

❀ ❀ ❀ ❀

Three weeks and four days later, we were on. I still wasn't apprised of all the details, but trusted in Pierce and Nola's thoroughness. They had seen through countless other risky missions as a duo, and they had plenty of help on this one.

At two-thirty in the morning, we landed the Hoverbug in a parking lot beside the boarded up concession stand near Tower 5. We chose Zuma Beach partly because of its expanse of parking lots. For Ecotrams and other ground transports, Doc Shaft procured a coded transponder that would raise the lot gates. Dozens of craft and vehicles were already there, others pulling and dropping in. People emerged carrying wood, ranging from a bundle of twigs, to a length of two-by-four, to a split log. I looked at Nola quizzically. "Weapons? No one said anything about weapons."

"Let's hope not," she said. "We're off to find the kit people. Take care of yourself, and over there by the tower are your buddies. Meet back at the bug if things get tetchy." She hugged me and kissed my cheek. I watched her and Pierce stroll out onto the sand, holding hands as if they were on a casual date.

It was a cool late November night, around seventy-five degrees, about as cool as it ever was anymore, and I was happy about my voluminous robe. The onshore breeze chilled the air a bit more than the usual dry Santa Ana. I walked toward the lifeguard tower, against which Phoebe and Terrence leaned. She struggled to keep her hood on her head in the wind, but finally just let it flop off. "The hell with it," she said. "I'm already breaking a shitload of other laws." Her hair was freshly, bluntly cut, springy as ever. I complimented her on her ever-glorious coif.

"Got all dolled up for the convocation," she said, and held out her hand.

Terrence held out his hand, and kissed me. It hadn't been so long since we'd kissed, and I leaned into it and lingered for a few seconds more.

"Don't make me the third wheel, sweethearts," Phoebe said, and with me in the middle, still holding hands, we sauntered over to where the crowd had begun to gather.

"Are you nuh-nuh-nuh-nervous?" Terrence asked.

I paused a beat before I said, "Surprisingly, no." I felt fine, even though it was the middle of the night and we were trespassing, in violation of curfew, gathering without a permit, and about to assist thousands—four was the estimate—in removing their government identification and communication devices.

Then I recalled we hadn't chosen Zuma simply because of the practical parking accommodations. We chose it because it had been part of our childhood, because the beaches had belonged to the public for decades, until all things benefiting the public became privatized, and all private information became public. How confounding it had been, years before, when people who claimed to be against big government bought it off, stuck it in their belts, and used it like a truncheon. What a clever disguise they had worn.

I wasn't nervous at all about taking back one beach and ourselves. That seemed like a downright modest robbery.

A young woman in wire-rimmed glasses that enlarged her sparkling eyes handed us our kits. I accepted mine as a souvenir because I sure as hell didn't need it. My device had been removed the hard way. I showed her the scar. "More power to us," the lovely young one said, and then to my friends, "Save your Dots for the fire." She filtered into the growing crowd.

I focused a pen light for Phoebe and Terrence while they stamped out their Dots, and pushed in the replacements. "Congratulations," I said. "You are now who you are." We walked down to the ocean and got our feet wet, even if it wasn't a Clear Beach Day. We had probably drunk tap water that was worse for us than the soothing brine we bathed our feet in.

"Did you hear we've been assigned a funky flat in the canyon, near Pierce and Nola?" Phoebe blinked and smiled with her eyes. "Within a few miles, I'm told. The three of us degenerates will be together again."

"Really?" I said, elated. "Those sneaky, conniving rascals."

"I've already wrapped and boxed my dry food and wine supplies. The move will come soon. Could be as soon as tomorrow, depending upon what happens today."

"Really?" I said. "What about your freezer, and all your furniture?"

"Remains to be seen. There's been mention of a vintage boxcar attached to a yurt. Don't know about freezer storage."

"Dibs on the yurt," Terrence said.

"Speak for yourself," I said, and kissed him on the ear. All of our hoods were blown off by now.

When we rejoined the others after what seemed a few minutes, the crowd had trebled and it was obvious the people carrying wood were not bearing weapons. They were fire makers. They'd dug a colossal pit in the sand and placed the smaller pieces at the bottom, dousing them with kerosene. About twenty feet in diameter, the pit erupted in an impressive blaze as the kindling lit. After it burned for a while, larger pieces were added to the flames. At this point, we heard Nola on a bullhorn, calmly directing everyone to use proper caution, but to cast their Dot devices ASAP into the fire.

I walked to the blaze with Phoebe and Terrence, and held onto their waists as they shed themselves of their Dots. We then moved away, back from the cordial crowd, who were yelling encouragements like, "Good riddance," and "Throw a coin, make a wish." There was a festival atmosphere, nothing too hilarious but more akin to a sigh of collective relief. We were doing something right. We were checking the sky for the glow strips of police craft, but we were going through with it anyway. So far no sign of them, but it wouldn't be long, no doubt. How they would handle a crowd as enormous and burgeoning as this one remained to be seen.

We sat by the guard tower, one at which Phoebe and Pierce's young father might have worked during summers long past, and we watched the proceedings. People of all different colors and sizes and ages and abilities pitched their government-issue entrapment into the inferno and melded their identities. There were even some children, I noted in wonder, since so few were brought into the world in present days. Their parents assisted with the Dot removal.

"Will it hurt, Mama?" one boy said, and she replied, "No, lovey. Not as much as if you keep it."

That was the moment. That was when I took in all of

the setting, and saw the fire glowing on the palm trees, on Phoebe's hair, on Terrence's fuzzy chest, on the faces of the children and adults who were here for one daring evening, glowing like the stardust and heat and light that made us. Everything that I had done, or not done, or that had been done to me—everything had brought me to this place, Theo, and it was not the end of the world.

We were all here together, and it was not the end of the world.

Acknowledgments

I would never have written the first novella of this book if not for the candor of my advisors and contemporaries at Vermont College, who told me I had too many characters to inhabit a short story then guided me through my leap into a longer genre. I'm deeply grateful for their insight and encouragement. Many thanks to Rosemary James and Joe DeSalvo of Pirate's Alley Faulkner Society and Faulkner House Books for awarding *Flashcards* the Faulkner Medal and treating me to a celebration in New Orleans. Chapters from the novella appeared in their magazine *Double Dealer Redux*, and also in *Other Voices*, and I appreciate the support of both periodicals. Years later, when the older, feistier Phoebe and Dessa returned to me as muses, Vicky Lettman and Carol Roan were kind enough to publish three chapters of the novella-in-progress in their anthology, *When Last on the Mountain*. Their faith in the project kept it alive. Mary Gunst and Esau Kerr helped me make my own writing retreat at their lovely Horizon Cottages in Westmorland, Jamaica where I completed *The Curse of Ambrosia*. I am forever thankful to them and their staff for a generous supply of solitude, Blue Mountain coffee, Red Stripe, soft-shell crab, and yellow snapper, not necessarily in that order.

A huge thank you to Elizabeth Searle, Suzzanne Kelley, Alan Davis, and everyone at New Rivers Press for selecting and publishing the book.

Many people have bolstered me over the years and inspired me to write a book about abiding friendship: my erudite, bighearted, and occasionally profane English teacher pals; the Bluebirds; the film salon gang; far-flung roommates and fellow wanderers—you know who you are, and all of you have by turns enriched and saved my life. Special thanks to Sara Kay Rupnik and Liz Abrams-Morley and our peripatetic band of scribes, Around the Block Writers Collaborative. Abundant thanks also to Karen Blackstone, self-dubbed human greeting card, and not the smarmy kind.

None of this would mean much without Andy, who taught me to trust.

About the Author

Tracy Robert, a native of Southern California, holds an MFA and has taught writing for three decades. She won the Pirate's Alley Faulkner Prize for Fiction, was a finalist for the Flannery O'Connor Award for Short Fiction, and has been published in various periodicals and anthologies, notably *Forever Sisters* (Pocket Books) and *When Last on the Mountain* (Holy Cow! Press). A co-founder of Around the Block Writers Collaborative, she facilitates writing retreats in Jamaica, Ireland, and Italy. This is her first book, winner of the Many Voices Project Prize in prose.

About New Rivers Press

New Rivers Press emerged from a drafty Massachusetts barn in winter 1968. Intent on publishing work by new and emerging poets, founder C. W. "Bill" Truesdale labored for weeks over an old Chandler & Price letterpress to publish three hundred fifty copies of Margaret Randall's collection, *So Many Rooms Has a House But One Roof.*

Nearly four hundred titles later, New Rivers, a non-profit and now teaching press based since 2001 at Minnesota State University Moorhead, has remained true to Bill's goal of publishing the best new literature—poetry and prose—from new, emerging, and established writers.

New Rivers Press authors range in age from twenty to eighty-nine. They include a silversmith, a carpenter, a geneticist, a monk, a tree-trimmer, and a rock musician. They hail from cities such as Christchurch, Honolulu, New Orleans, New York City, Northfield (Minnesota), and Prague.

Charles Baxter, one of the first authors with New Rivers, calls the press "the hidden backbone of the American literary tradition." Continuing this tradition, in 1981 New Rivers began to sponsor the Minnesota Voices Project (now called Many Voices Project) competition. It is one of the oldest literary competitions in the United States, bringing recognition and attention to emerging writers. Other New Rivers publications include the American Fiction Series, the American Poetry Series, New Rivers Abroad, and the Electronic Book Series.

Please visit our website newriverspress.com for more information.

Many Voices Project Award Winners

("OP" indicates that the paper copy is out of print; "e-book" indicates that the title is available as an electronic publication.)

#132 *Home Studies,* Julie Gard (e-book)

#131 *Flashcards and The Curse of Ambrosia,* Tracy Robert (e-book)

#130 *Dispensations,* Randolph Thomas (e-book)

#129 *Invasives,* Brandon Krieg

#128 *Whitney,* Joe Stracci (e-book)

#127 *Rare Earth,* Bradford Tice

#126 *The Way of All Flux,* Sharon Suzuki-Martinez

#125 *It Takes You Over,* Nick Healy (e-book)

#124 *The Muse of Ocean Parkway and Other Stories,* Jacob Lampart (e-book)

#123 *Hotel Utopia,* Robert Miltner

#122 *Kinesthesia,* Stephanie N. Johnson

#121 *Birds of Wisconsin,* B.J. Best

#120 *At Home Anywhere,* Mary Hoffman (e-book)

#119 *Friend Among Stones,* Maya Pindyck

#118 *Fallibility,* Elizabeth Oness

#117 *When Love Was Clean Underwear,* Susan Barr-Toman (e-book)

#116 *The Sound of It,* Tim Nolan

#115 *Hollow Out,* Kelsea Habecker

#114 *Bend from the Knees,* Benjamin Drevlow

#113 *The Tender, Wild Things,* Diane Jarvenpa

#112 *Signaling for Rescue,* Marianne Herrmann

#111 *Cars Go Fast,* John Chattin

#110 *Terrain Tracks,* Purvi Shah

#109 *Numerology and Other Stories,* Christian Michener

#108 *Not a Matter of Love,* Beth Alvarado (e-book)

#107 *Real Karaoke People,* Ed Bok Lee

#106 *Love in An Expanding Universe,* Ron Rindo

#105 *Second Language,* Ronna Wineberg (e-book)

#104 *Landing Zones,* Edward Micus

#103 *The Volunteer,* Candace Black

#102 *Nice Girls and Other Stories,* Cezarija Abartis

#101 *Paper Boat,* Cullen Bailey Burns

#99 *Mozart's Carriage,* Daniel Bachhuber

#98 *The Pact*, Walter Roers

#97 *Alone with the Owl*, Alan Davis

#96 *Rafting on the Water Table*, Susan Steger Welsh

#95 *Woman Lake*, Richard Broderick

#94 *The Record Player and Other Stories*, Winifred Moranville

#93 *Casting Lines*, Orval Lund

#92 *Dakota Incarnate: A Collection of Short Stories*,
    Bill McDonald

#91 *Vendettas, Charms, and Prayers*, Pamela Gemin

#90 *An Alchemy in the Bones*, William Reichard

#89 *Music of the Inner Lakes*, Roger Sheffer

#88 *The Fragile Peace You Keep*, Kel Munger

#87 *The Dirty Shame Hotel and Other Stories*, Ron Block

#85 *Sermon on a Perfect Spring Day*, Philip Bryant (e-book)

#84 *Rootbound*, Jeanne Emmons

#83 *Bonfire*, Connie Wanek

#82 *Laundromat Blues*, Lupe Solis

#81 *The Natural Father*, Robert Lacy

#80 *Self Storage*, Mary Helen Stefaniak

#79 *Fishing for Myth*, Heid E. Erdrich

#78 *Sustenance*, Aaron Anstett

#77 *On the Road to Patsy Cline*, John Reinhard

#76 *Remembering China 1935-1945*, Bea Exner Liu

#75 *The Dance Hall at Spring Hill*, Duke Klassen (e-book)

#74 *Divining the Landscape*, Diane Jarvenpa

#73 *To Collect the Flesh*, Greg Hewett

#72 *Heathens*, David Haynes

#71 *Secrets Men Keep*, Ron Rindo

#70 *Everything's a Verb*, Debra Marquart

#69 *Revealing the Unknown to a Pair of Lovers*,
    Ann Lundberg Grunke

#68 *What They Always Were*, Norita Dittberner-Jax

#67 *Coming Up for Light and Air*, Barbara Crow

#66 *Mal D'Afrique*, Jarda Cervenka (e-book)

#65 *Aerial Studies*, Sandra Adelmund Witt

#64 *The Peace Terrorist*, Carol Masters

#63 *Thin Ice and Other Risks*, Gary Eller

#62 *Falling in Love at the End of the World*, Rick Christman

#61 *This House Is Filled With Cracks*, Madelyn Camrud

#60 *Handmade Paper*, Patricia Barone

#59 *Under the Influence of Blackbirds*, Sharon Van Sluys

#58 *Jump Rope Queen*, Karen Loeb

#57 *Wolves*, Jim Johnson

#56 *The Second Thing I Remember*, Judith Hougen

#55 *Right by My Side*, David Haynes (OP; e-book)

#54 *Rumors from the Lost World*, Alan Davis (e-book)

#53 *Edith Jacobson Begins to Fly*, Patricia Zontelli

#52 *Learning to Dance & Other Stories*, Sharon Oard Warner

#51 *Mykonos: A Memoir* , Nancy Raeburn (OP)

#50 *Billy Brazil*, Emilio DeGrazia (OP)

#49 *House Fire: A Collection of Poems*, B.J. Buhrow

#48 *From the Lanai & Other Hawaii Stories*, Jessica K. Saiki

#47 *Pictures of Three Seasons*, Gail Rixen

#46 *Pieces from the Long Afternoon*, Monica Ochtrup

#45 *Primary Colors*, Barbara Croft

#44 *But I Won't Go Out in a Boat*, Sharon Chmielarz

#43 *No Peace at Versailles and Other Stories*, Nina Barragan

#42 *Borrowed Voices*, Roger Sheffer

#41 *This Body She's Entered*, Mary K. Rummel

#40 *Suburban Metaphysics*, Ron Rindo

#39 *Out Far, In Deep*, Alvin Handelman

#38 *Dismal River*, Ronald Block

#37 *Turning Out the Lights*, Sigrid Bergie

#36 *The Transparency of Skin*, Catherine Stearns (OP)

#35 *Burning the Prairie*, John Reinhard

#34 *Last Summer*, Davida Kilgore (OP)

#33 *The High Price of Everything*, Kathleen Coskran

#32 *Storm Lines*, Warren Woessner (OP)

#31 *Dying Old and Dying Young*, Susan Williams

#30 *Once, A Lotus Garden*, Jessica Saiki (OP)

#28 *The Wind*, Patricia Barone

#27 *All Manner of Monks*, Benet Tvedten (OP)

#26 *Flash Paper*, Theresa Pappas (OP)

#25 *Tap Dancing for Big Mom*, Roseann Lloyd

#24 *Twelve Below Zero*, Anthony Bukoski (OP)

#23 *Locomotion*, Elizabeth Evans (OP)

#22 *What I Cannot Say*, *I Will Say*, Monica Ochtrup

#21 *Descent of Heaven Over the Lake*, Sheryl Noethe (OP)

#20 *Matty's Heart*, C.J. Hribal (OP)

#19 *Stars Above, Stars Below*, Margaret Hasse (OP)

#18 *Golf Ball Diver*, Neal Bowers (OP)

#17 *The Weird Kid*, Mark Vinz (OP)

#16 *Morning Windows*, Michael Moos (OP)

#15 *Powers*, Marisha Chamberlain (OP)

#14 *Suspicious Origins*, Perry Glasser (OP)

#13 *Blenheim Palace*, Wendy Parrish (OP)

#12 *Rivers, Stories, Houses, Dreams*, Madelon Sprengnether

#11 *We'll Come When It Rains*, Yvette Nelson (OP)

#10 *Different Arrangements*, Sharon Chmielarz

#9 *Casualties*, Katherine Carlson

#8 *Night Sale*, Richard Broderick

#7 *When I Was a Father*, Alvaro Carona-Hine (OP)

#6 *Changing the Past*, Laurie Taylor (OP)

#5 *I Live in the Watchmaker's Town*, Ruth Roston (OP)

#4 *Normal Heart*, Madelon Gohlke (OP)

#3 *Heron Dancer*, John Solensten

#2 *The Reconstruction of Light*, John Minczeski (OP)

#1 *Household Wounds*, Deborah Keenan (OP)